THE VANISHING MAN

Popular novelist and secret agent Alec Black is on an undercover mission on Mars. The Martian colonists are preparing for a major offensive against earth and someone is stirring up war-fever. Black must try to prevent it, or the whole system will be engulfed in atomic war. When Black finds himself shadowed by a man who, when confronted, vanishes into thin air, his investigation turns into his strangest case and very soon he's plunged into a dimension of horror . . .

SYDNEY J. BOUNDS

THE VANISHING MAN

Complete and Unabridged

LINFORD
Leicester

First published in Great Britain

First Linford Edition
published 2010

British Library CIP Data

Bounds, Sydney J.
    The vanishing man. - -
    (Linford mystery library)
    1. Space warfare- -Fiction.
    2. Mars (Planet)- -Fiction.
    3. Science fiction.
    4. Large type books.
    I. Title II. Series
    823.9′14–dc22

    ISBN 978–1–44480–418–8

1

Vital mission

The girl with bright green hair was sitting on a high stool against the glittering chromium and plastic bar, sipping from a tall cone of glass. I looked at her for a long moment as I went through the swing door of the Marsport bar. Behind me, flat concrete stretched for miles, the rocket landing site, with administrative buildings close at hand. The fuelling and engineering hangars were a little way off. I heard a runabout car hum past the door, the clatter of feet of hurrying people.

The barroom was shaped like a horseshoe, patterned with gay tables whose colours were the crude, harsh colours that they like on Mars. There weren't many people in the bar. I let my eyes rove, exploring, summing up. It was quiet, and I wasn't expecting any trouble yet.

The girl's bright green hair fell in luxuriant coils to her shoulders.

I smiled a little, wondering why she should so easily catch my eye. Maybe it was the green hair — which I supposed must be the latest fashion. She was wearing a green dress of some light and airy material. The neckline was fastened by an emerald clasp. Her feet were dainty and shod with high-heeled sandals.

I crossed to the bar and hoisted myself onto the stool next to her. The barman looked suspiciously at me.

I said: 'Something tall and cool — an Earth drink.'

He almost spat his disgust.

'Earthman!'

He gave me a look I didn't enjoy, but he served me. I sipped the drink, wondering if trouble was coming earlier than I anticipated.

The girl with green hair swung round to take a close look at me. The way she turned made me wonder if she were pliable, like a rubber doll. She had a smooth oval face with a clear skin, tanned, and eyes of a copper colour. Her chin was determined.

She smiled in a friendly way, and said:

'Don't take any notice. I like Earthmen. They have more money to spend.'

I smiled back.

'You're one Mars girl I could fall for without any bother. May I buy you a drink?'

Her eyes studied me over the rim of her glass. She emptied it. 'Why not? I'll have the same again,' she said.

The barman refilled her glass. I paid, without tipping him. She smiled her thanks.

We sat there, watching each other. It was like cat and mouse and I had a feeling I was the mouse. I pulled myself together. I had a job to do. I should be the cat . . .

She said, abruptly: 'You're Alexander Black, aren't you? I'm Sadie Lubinski. I know, Lubinski's quite a mouthful, so it's all right to call me Sadie. Everyone does. It's wonderful meeting you like this, Mr. Black, by chance.'

My scalp prickled. By chance? I wondered about that. An uneasy tremor ran right through me. Suppose there had been a leakage?

'Just how did you know me, Sadie?'

She answered, too quickly, I thought.

'I've seen your picture. On the back of one of your books, I think.'

'Of course,' I smiled. But though most authors have their photographs printed I'd been careful to avoid that mistake. In my job, you can't be too careful about things like that. She had received her information from another source . . .

But I had to play the part of a writer of space-adventure stories. 'You like my stuff?' I said.

Her eyes lit up. She became enthusiastic. She laid it on with a trowel.

'I do! I've read every one of your stories, Alec. And not just on a screen, either. I even buy your actual book editions — I prefer them. You don't mind if I call you Alec?' I signified that was all right by me. She went on: 'You have such a fast-moving style, I'm carried right away. I'll never forget the battle with the aliens from another system in *Peril on Pluto*. Nor that exciting moment, in

Miners of Mercury, when you left the hero suspended by a thin cord over a volcano. And your love interest is always so convincing — I thought that final scene, in *Rings of Saturn*, between Eve and the captain, was absolutely thrilling. Tell me, do you write out of your own experience?'

Remembering that scene from *Rings of Saturn*, I fingered my collar. It had been one of my more lurid efforts.

'I dramatize those things a little,' I admitted modestly.

She looked disappointed.

'You're quite handsome,' she pointed out. 'Just like one of your own heroes!'

I thought that was going too far. I'll admit to being not unhandsome, and with having a certain success with the ladies, but I'm no fictional glamour boy. For one thing, I'm not tall enough, and my features are a little rugged. I'm wiry and athletic — you have to keep in trim for my job — but no one ever swooned at the sight of me.

Sadie fished around among the multitudinous contents of her plastic handbag.

She brought out a book, my latest epic.

'I wonder,' she said softly, 'if you'd autograph this for me?'

It was too pat. No one carries around a copy of *Death on Deimos* in the hope of meeting the author by chance. I wondered if she'd read it. Taking the book in one hand and a stylo in the other, I scribbled across the title page:

> *To the loveliest girl on Mars,*
> *A goddess with green hair,*
> *From her sincere admirer,*
> *Alec.*

Her eyes widened in pleasure. Her voice was warm.

'You don't mean that,' she said. 'I'll bet you write the same in every girl's book.'

'I mean it,' I told her.

'I suppose you visit the planets you write about?' she asked.

I nodded.

'I like to get my background material right. Makes a story sound authentic.'

'Then,' she pounced, scoring a small

6

point, 'You're going to write a book about Mars?'

I admitted she was right. That was supposed to be my intention; to write a story set on Mars. And I was there to collect local colour. On the surface, that sounded all right; it was a good cover, but did it take her in? Just how much did Sadie know about me?

'If you like,' she offered, 'I'll show you around. It would be fun for me, and — '

'Fun for me, too,' I grinned.

If she was who I thought she was, and if she guessed my real purpose in coming to Mars, her company was going to be embarrassing. But to object would have been out of character with the part I had to play.

'I'll take you up on that,' I said.

The bar was getting noisy. More people had come in and an argument was starting. I tensed, waiting. Perhaps Sadie had only been keeping me there for the trouble that was to come.

A young man with a shock of yellow hair was talking loudest. He gave his opinions with an air of one who has had the party line rammed down his throat until he believed he had thought of it himself.

' — the only way is force,' he was saying with fervour. 'Force is all they understand. All right, we'll give 'em force. Teach the tyrants we can stand up to them. Show 'em we're tired of being pushed around. Who do they think they are, ordering us around? We're Martians, and this is our planet. We'll fight, and go on fighting. That's the way to get rid of the yoke of Earth — the only way!'

He spat contemptuously, to give emphasis to his rhetoric. I kept calm, sipped my drink. Although Yellow-hair had his back to me, I knew he was talking for my benefit, trying to draw me into a quarrel.

He continued fiercely: 'If it means war, well, there are worse things than war. Slavery, and tyranny, and bowing down to armchair dictators on Earth. This is Mars, our planet, the planet our ancestors pioneered without help from the Terran government. Why should we pay taxes to Earth? Why should we let them tell us how to run our planet? I tell you, I'm sick of it.'

Some of the crowd agreed noisily. I got one or two cold looks. Still I kept quiet.

'I don't want war and bloodshed and death — none of us do,' the young man went on. 'All we want is peace, to be left alone to live in peace. But they won't leave us alone. Mars is being strangled by red tape. All right, if they want war, they can have it! We've the spaceships, and the atom bombs. I say again, if Earth wants war, let 'em have it. Wipe out the tyrants. Clean the system of all traces of Earth's power. A free Mars for a free people!'

He got a cheer for that. I glanced at Sadie, but her face remained blank. Across the room, a man sat with his back to me, glaring into a mirror. He was watching me, all right. I felt the tension grow. It was like being submerged in a sea of hatred — and I was the only Earthman in the bar. If it came to a fight, I could expect no help.

Yellow-hair was still at it, working up race-hatred against Earth. He knew what he was doing, and made a good job of it.

I promised myself five minutes alone with that young man one day. Of course, he was talking rubbish, but from the effect it had you'd have thought they were all chained slaves with a taskmaster standing over them, whip in hand.

True, Earth had been pretty high-handed with the first settlers on Mars, but the colony had grown and power had equalized. True, there was still a minority on Earth who thought of the red planet as an outpost. But the government had a more enlightened attitude towards the colonies now, so this trouble was fed on hot air. That made it none-the-less dangerous, and my job . . .

I remembered my chief. A quiet man, the chief, with a quiet voice that made his statement all the more terrible.

'I'm sending you to Mars, Alec. I don't know what it's about, but trouble's brewing, serious trouble. War. Someone is working up war-fever and unless some-thing drastic is done to stop it, the whole system will be engulfed in the bloodiest war our race has known. Reports come into my office every day, reports that indicate preparations for a major offensive against Earth. We would win in the end, but many people would die before peace came again. I'm giving you the job of stopping that.'

I remembered the feeling I had, excitement mixed up with a sense of personal achievement, and humility. The job was bigger than me.

'I'm sending you, Alec, because you've proved yourself to be one of my best operatives — that, and the fact you have achieved a certain amount of popularity as a writer. It may shield you from immediate danger and give you time to act.'

It's true I had got results where older, more experienced men had fallen down; but I'd had luck so far. I hoped it would continue.

The chief finished: 'Remember, your job is to prevent war, not start it. You must do nothing that will precipitate an outbreak. That's all — and good luck.'

Yellow-hair was still talking and the atmosphere in the bar definitely anti-Earth. I pressed Sadie's hand, and said, loudly:

'I'll see you home.'

She rose at once, and I was surprised to find that she just reached to my shoulder. Somehow, I'd thought her taller. The man who had been watching me in the mirror left his table and crossed to the door. He went outside.

But I wasn't getting away as easily as that. Yellow-hair turned, glaring hatred at me. He demanded:

'Well, Earthman, have you anything to say in your defence? Are you going to stand there and pretend ignorance of your government's actions? Do you deny us the right to be free men?'

He was magnificent. He had the crowd with him, all the way. The door looked a thousand miles away and the crowd was ready to trample me into the ground. It was a tricky moment. My natural instinct was to stand up for Earth, to call Yellow-hair's bluff. 'Do nothing to pre-cipitate an outbreak,' the chief had said. I swallowed my pride. A secret agent has to do that often — and I was supposed to be a writer of space adventure stories.

I assumed a calmness I did not feel.

I said: 'I completely agree with everything you've just said. The Terran government is tyrannical and the only thing you can do is fight back.'

There was dead silence. Yellow-hair looked as if he couldn't believe his ears. Obviously, I should have been goaded into action; and the argument would have led to a fight. My words knocked him off-balance.

In the hush, I took Sadie's arm and walked to the door. A muttering of angry, cheated voices followed me, but I didn't turn. Someone called: 'All Earthmen are cowards!' I kept going. It wasn't till the door swung shut behind me that I felt easier; somehow, I'd half-expected a knife in the back.

Luckily, a runabout was cruising past and I hailed the driver, anxious to get away before Yellow-hair thought of coming after me. Sadie got in the back and gave the driver her address. It was then I noticed the other car, parked across the way; the man behind the wheel was the same man who had been watching me in the mirror.

I frowned, not liking the idea of being

followed. 'Wait,' I told the driver, and crossed the street. I studied my watcher closely as I approached. He was a small man, in a grey suit, so ordinary-looking as to be inconspicuous. A man with pale, nondescript features, a nonentity who would pass unnoticed in a crowd. An ideal shadow — but right now he wasn't in a crowd and so I saw him clearly.

It was a wide street and took a little time to cross. The runabout was large, oval-shaped on six wheels, the top a glassite hood for full visibility. A side window was open.

Another car passed, with its siren sounding a warning. I stood, waiting. Then went on. I reached the car belonging to the small, nondescript man, and started:

'Just what — '

My words slurred into silence. My mouth hung open. *The car was empty.*

I didn't believe it. I stuck my head in through the open window. It was roomy inside, with nowhere for a man to hide. I stood back, looking at the street. Empty. The small man had disappeared as completely as if he had never been there.

Only he had. I stared at the runabout as if expecting it to vanish too. It was a bad moment, and, suddenly, I knew what fear really was.

2

The mob

A cold sweat gathered on my forehead. I felt moisture crawl slowly down my left cheek. My hands were shaking and my legs seemed to have turned to jelly. Fear held me motionless, staring at the empty street and the empty car.

I've been in tight comers before, where my life hung by a single thread, but I'd never before felt as bad as I did at that moment. The unknown had touched me and the carefully built-up facade of civilization fell away and left me naked before something I could not understand. From a distance, I heard Sadie calling:

'Alec. What's wrong?'

Her voice brought me out of the shock. I turned away, using a tissue to wipe the sweat from my face. I was careful not to look back at that frighteningly empty car as I climbed into the seat beside Sadie. I was afraid I might see the small man again.

The driver of our hired runabout started his motor. We moved off. After a while, I found sufficient courage to look back. The road was empty. I was not being followed.

Sadie was curious. She asked:

'What happened back there?'

I tried to pass it off.

'Oh, nothing much. I thought I recognized someone. I was wrong — made a mistake, that's all.'

I was glad she didn't probe further. I was trying not to think of a small man who had vanished in front of my eyes. That was something I didn't like to think about.

The drive was a long one, through the wide avenues of Marsport, out to the residential suburbs, but I was so upset I hardly saw anything of the colony. Sadie was silent for a long time, then she nestled closer and slipped her hand into mine.

'You're the most unromantic writer of love stories I can imagine,' she told me.

I made an effort to relax. I glanced sideways at Sadie and, all at once, it didn't seem any effort at all. She was using one of those subtle perfumes; I hadn't noticed it before, but, in the car, close as we were, it grew on me. It was an exciting scent.

'Alec, this can't develop into anything — serious. You know that, don't you?'

I lay back in the pneumatic seat.

'Why not?' I challenged. 'I like you.'

She sighed, looked out of the window, then turned back to me. Her copper-coloured eyes held a wistful expression.

'It's impossible while Earth and Mars are, well, not on friendly terms.'

I said, harshly: 'Don't be afraid of the word. It's war you're thinking of.'

She nodded.

'Yes, we may well be at war in a short time, your planet and mine. If only Earth — '

I caught up her hand and pressed it.

'Earth doesn't want war,' I said. 'I have a feeling it will all blow over. Let's forget it now.' I drew her closer. 'Personally, I'm keen to improve Terran-Martian friend-ship!'

She didn't get the double meaning. To her, I was a spy for Earth, a man she had to watch. I was just a job, and not a pleasant one at that. I began to wonder what she really thought of me.

The car stopped outside a prefabricated bungalow that looked both smart and efficient. She gave me a visiphone number to call the next day, and left. I sat in the runabout, watching her walk towards the bungalow, with a graceful swing in the light Martian gravity. She looked as sleek as a well-fed member of the feline genus.

She let herself into the bungalow without looking back at me, and the door closed. I told the driver to take me to my hotel. The runabout started again, and, this time, I observed some of the view.

Marsport had grown from a city contained within an impenetrable glassite hemisphere. Now it was a collection of transparent bubbles, all interlinked by covered ways; the atmosphere of the planet, too thin and poisonous to humans, was filtered and augmented to Earth-normal before being pumped through the city. The protective dome, whilst allowing the weak sunlight to get through, also filtered out the ultra-violet and cosmic radiation that penetrated the thin Martian atmosphere. The rows of same-looking houses were laid out in orderly lanes; there were residential suburbs and an industrial centre, government and executive domes, a business quarter, a shopping and recreational centre. It was one vast hive of human activity.

The car bypassed a park where exotic flowers bloomed and a fountain sprayed rainbow-coloured water. Tall buildings studded with windows, which glittered like gems loomed ahead beyond the bungalow town. There was light and colour and noise. An orchestra played in the open, filling the air with the reedy sounds of a Martian fantasia. Men at a political meeting waved gaudy banners and shouted abuse at the tyranny of Earthmen.

I thought of Sadie, and the job I had to do, and the small man who vanished. Thinking of him, I shivered. It was the first truly alien touch I had found in Marsport; even after three generations, the descendants of the original colonists from Earth seemed only to have changed in the most superficial manner. They still loved and hated and ran the gamut of emotions known for centuries on Earth. But a man who could disappear right under my nose was something again.

My driver seemed to be taking a different route on the return journey. We passed through a squalid area, where silent factories were close packed and the streets narrow and ill-lit. Part of the early settlement, abandoned and ready for demolition preparatory to rebuilding along lines more in sympathy with the new Marsport.

Somewhere ahead, a hubbub of voices started. Angry voices, ranting about freedom and throwing off the yoke of Earth. I seemed to have heard it all before. There was a crowd on the street, blocking our path. The runabout slowed to a standstill.

I remained seated, expecting the driver to turn back. Instead, he got out and jerked open the door of my compartment.

'Outside,' he said, tersely. 'I'm not getting mobbed for carrying an Earthman. That'll be ten credits.'

I breathed hard, but it was no use arguing. The man was scared of the mob. I got out and handed over the credit bills. Stragglers from the crowd had already reached us. I heard hate-filled voices raised against me.

'An Earthman!'

'Get him — show the swine we mean business. Make an example of him!'

I started to walk quickly away. A hand caught my jacket sleeve. I brushed it off and hurried on, repressing a desire to run. I didn't want the mob howling at my heels and I was afraid that was what would happen if I made a bolt for it. There's nothing like showing fear to start a mob hunting.

Another man cut across my path. I started to go round him, wishing to avoid violence. He stepped directly in front of me, grinning, raising his arms to stop me going on. For a moment I stood still.

I said, very carefully: 'I've no quarrel

with you. I'm not interfering in the affairs of your planet. Please let me pass.'

He was a burly individual, taller than me, obviously stronger. He thought so, too.

'We know how to deal with Earthmen,' he said.

I stepped back a pace as he came at me, glancing round. The mass of the crowd was almost on top of us. I hadn't long to save myself. I had to make a decision quickly. He made it for me. His fist came for my face like a lump of granite at the end of a pile driver.

Automatically, I swayed sideways. His fist passed over my shoulder and I grabbed his arm. In my job you need to know something about unarmed combat. I pulled him clean over my shoulder. He described an arc through the air and hit the ground with sufficient force to discourage any interest he might have in immediate events.

Behind me, the grating of metal sounded. I turned. The runabout I had used was lying on its side and the driver had disappeared. A shout went up:

'The Earthman's killed one of us. Get him. Beat him into the ground. Kill . . . kill . . . kill . . . '

I didn't like the sound of that. It was a chant, rhythmic, terrible.

'*Kill . . . kill . . . kill*!'

I started to run. There was nothing else I could do and I place some value on my neck. The hunt was on. The crowd surged after me, running, shouting, brandishing fists and weapons. One man, to the front of the mob, carried a rope in which he fashioned a noose. I didn't need anyone to tell me what that was for. Someone had been reading up on the old-time lynching parties we had on Earth. I ran faster.

There was an intersection, and I took the street to the left because the lighting was weaker. Maybe if I could find a dark corner, I could hide. The crowd was swelling. There had been about twenty men in the crowd to start with; there had been thirty when I took to my heels. Now there must be fifty, and more joining it every minute. And not all men, either. I saw the hate-burning eyes of women in the crowd. One woman waved a large carving knife; the naked blade glinted ominously.

Apart from a slight lead, I had one advantage. The Martians were all garbed in bright colours, reds and greens and blues that jarred nightmarishly. Crude, harsh colours. My own nylon suit was dark grey. If I found a place to hide, I'd see them before they saw me.

Shadowy figures came out from side turnings. I had to change course several times, Somewhere a drum was beating a monotonous rhythm, insidiously working up the blood lust of the crowd. I sweated, grimly piling on speed. It's one thing to enjoy a chase while seated in a comfortable chair in front of a Tri-D screen; quite another to be at the wrong end of a hunt in real life. I knew now what it felt like to be a stag running before the pack. It wasn't a nice feeling.

The drum was beating louder, insistently, calling more Martians to join in the chase that was intended to end with my death. I've heard the throb of drums before, but nothing like that. It got in my blood, went round and round inside my head. My legs worked in rhythm to its pounding, and the mob ran behind, shouting like wild animals. They couldn't be sane, I thought; no human being could behave like this.

Somehow their humanity had been repressed and a blood-frenzy instilled in its place. I couldn't think how, but I knew this hatred of Earth had been deliberately manufactured; and the Martians were transformed into an unthinking mob designed for mass murder. The drum part of it, but not all. No drumbeat, no matter how terrible, could reduce men to animals. Something else was involved, some diabolical weapon that I could not imagine.

I was sweating and breathless, tiring fast. Doubts crowded in on me and I wasn't feeling so sure of myself. I had to find asylum before the mob tore me limb from limb. Then, down a narrow alley, the entrance of a derelict warehouse waited to receive me. I went in, searching for darkness and shadow, a place to rest in safety.

Behind me, the crowd started to chant again: '*Kill . . . kill . . . kill!*'

They were throwing stones and bricks, and one grazed my head, drawing blood. I felt the sticky stuff creep down my face, felt the sharpness of pain. I was running zigzag across a litter of fallen struts, threading a drunken course through debris. A high wall, half-roofed over, threw deep shadow. I caught a glimpse of a metal girder jutting out above my head . . . I ran for it, springing upward.

The light gravity aided me. My hands caught, held, and for a moment I was dangling in space. Then I swung my body up and my legs twined round the cold metal. I heaved myself onto the girder and wriggled along its length. There was a hollow where it joined the wall, a hollow large enough for me to crawl in and lay flat. I hoped no one had seen my acrobatic effort.

I lay there, panting, sweat soaking me. The noise increased as the mob came howling closer. I saw a mass of garish colour, heard the pounding of heavy feet, the rhythm of the drum. The chant swelled in crescendo.

'Kill . . . kill . . . *kill* . . . '

They were right under me now, a horde of mad people streaming past. Their faces were horrible, their mouths working, their eyes alight with the lust to kill. It was like watching a crowd of robots run amok. Fortunately none of them looked up as they passed under the girder where I crouched; they passed me by, and the sound died away as they went on, searching further into the chaos of derelict buildings.

I waited till the last of the mob was out of sight then dropped silently to the ground. I ran back the way I had come, away from the mob. Presently, I came out on a lighted street, and slowed to a walk. I walked fast, looking for a runabout that would take me clear of the danger zone. I never wanted to meet anything like that again.

Someone stepped from a doorway and took my arm. I stopped. It was the uniform that prevented me from taking offensive action. I saw a blue uniform glittering with gold and silver, and an official badge.

I breathed easier — so there was some law in Marsport.

The policeman said: 'Just what do you think you're doing?'

I grinned weakly.

'Saving my neck!'

He looked at me coldly.

'An Earthman, are you? You ought to have more sense than to be in this part of the city. I've a good mind to charge you with starting a riot. Let's see your papers.'

I realized I was going to get little sympathy from him. He might be a policeman and his duty to keep the peace, but he was Martian — and he was on the side of the crowd. I produced my official papers.

He looked through them and handed them back.

'They seem to be in order.'

He sounded disappointed.

I said: 'Don't you think you might do something about that mob? Or is it in order for the people of Marsport to hunt an Earthman? They weren't going to play kiss-in-the-ring if they caught me.'

I suppose I put more venom into my

tone than I intended. He frowned his disapproval.

'The police are understaffed for this kind of work. Naturally, we try to maintain order — but the people here are excitable and, at present, there is a considerable anti-Earth feeling. It is not easy to control a large crowd.'

'That's all very well,' I said. 'But you should check this bad feeling at source. No good waiting till it breaks out.'

He shrugged his indifference to my suggestion, then took a reed whistle from his pocket and piped on it.

'You'll get official transport out of this area,' he said, briefly.

I waited, feeling easier in my mind; but still there was a nagging doubt that he would act on my behalf if the mob came back. He could easily have slipped away and pretended ignorance of my danger; and I shouldn't be in a position to put my case before the people who mattered. A corpse doesn't answer back.

So I sighed with relief when the police runabout cruised down the street and stopped beside us.

'An Earthman,' my policeman said. 'Take him home before we have murder on our hands.'

I got in the car and gave the name of my hotel. We moved off, travelling down wide, brightly-lit avenues. I relaxed. I was safe for the moment, but for how long? The chief had been right about trouble brewing, but even he underestimated the seriousness of the situation. I began to wonder what I could do about it.

The police car dropped me off at my hotel. I went straight to my room. My travelling bag stood in one corner. I opened it and checked the contents; nothing was missing, but the careful order of things had been upset. Someone had searched my belongings while I'd been absent. I smiled. There was nothing in it to indicate I was more than a writer of space-adventure stories. Someone had wasted his time.

I undressed, ready for bed, wondering if the trap had been deliberate! If Sadie had known of it. I slept.

3

Desert trip

I rose late, breakfasted off Martian fruit juice and green-corn bread, and used the hotel visiphone to call Sadie. The screen remained blank and no answering voice came. After two minutes a stereotyped message lit up:

YOUR PARTY IS NOT AVAILABLE. PLEASE DISENGAGE AND CALL BACK LATER.

I left the visiphone booth with a feeling of satisfaction. Sadie might be out or just playing hard-to-get; whatever the reason for her not answering my call, I now had an excuse for going off on my own without departing from the character role I had to play. And there were things I wanted to do and see without having Sadie around.

I walked out of the hotel and ignored the line of cars for hire. I turned left and walked casually through the morning crowds on the boulevards. The scene never changed. There was the vast dome high overhead, concrete and steel and plastic structures; the men and women in garishly-coloured clothes. There was only weak sunlight, augmented by artificial lights; no rain, no fresh air, no change of any sort. Marsport is self-contained, completely artificial.

I walked slowly, trying to gather impressions of the scene. No one bothered me. The first thing that struck me was the low percentage of Earth people. That disturbed me; it was unusual, because Terrans have a habit of being where there's profit to be made. Mars was a planet rich in mineral wealth, a world where great development was possible. It was a world ready for exploitation, and the small number of Earthmen was unnatural and alarming. I found myself wondering if, in some way, they had been scared off. No one would want to be caught on Mars if war broke out.

It was easy to pick them out — and

difficult to say how. Superficially, there's no difference between people from the home planet and the colonists. You couldn't say that all Martians wore bright clothes or had tanned skins, or were taller or leaner. It wasn't as easy as that. The difference was more subtle, hard to define, but quite definite. You couldn't mistake an Earthman on Mars or a colonial on Earth.

I kept walking, observing the casual scene and thinking it over, till I reached the building I wanted. It was tall and majestic, set in a park where flowers bloomed and strange fish swam in a circular pond. The bronze plaque was small and dignified and used small, neat lettering:

TERRAN EMBASSY

I went up the steps to the tiled reception room and gave the clerk my name. I didn't have to wait long. An usher took me up in a lift and showed me into a large room, austerely furnished, where the resident ambassador waited to see me.

His name was Ross. He was slim, middle-aged, dressed in formal black. We shook hands and he said:

'I expected you yesterday, Mr. Black. I was notified of your arrival.'

He had a smooth tongue and a smooth manner, but, underneath it, there was worry.

I said: 'I got held up,' and told him about Sadie and how near I'd come to a sticky end. I omitted to mention the small man who vanished; I didn't want to be shipped back to Earth listed mentally unstable.

Ross commented: 'We know about the woman Lubinski. We can't be certain, of course, but in all probability she's an agent for the Martian government.'

He picked up a message-form from his desk and waved it at me.

'From the police department. I've already been informed of your little escapade. Personally, Mr. Black, I can only say that you had a very lucky escape — I hope you'll be more careful in future.'

'I will,' I said, but he missed the irony

in my voice. I never have liked politicians. But I was there to cooperate with Ross so I kept my thoughts to myself.

He continued: 'May I impress on you the importance of refraining from any action which may cause strain between my department and the Martian government?'

'You may,' I told him.

He looked at me carefully; I could tell he thought I was too young for the job, that someone with more experience should have been sent. It wouldn't have mattered. Intelligence personnel and politicians never see eye-to-eye over methods. There's always that icy-cold reluctance to cooperate, the distrust that one department has about another's capabilities.

'The situation here is tense,' Ross said. 'There can be no doubt that the Martians are planning war against Earth. No doubt whatever. Someone is working up war fever very efficiently. Your job is to find that someone and stop him. You have carte blanche, of course, but in the event of your being caught in the act of espionage, you understand that you can expect no help from us. We must decline all knowledge of your activities.'

'Naturally.' This was old stuff to me. A spy is no one's friend when he's caught.

'Sadie Lubinski was expecting me,' I said, leaning forward. 'How many of your people here knew I was coming? There's been a leakage somewhere.'

Ross stiffened. His voice was very cold.

'Myself only. I decode all secret messages personally. I can assure you I have not revealed your identity.'

I nodded, puzzled. It seemed unlikely there had been a leak at our end. That was something to check. The chief would take care of it.

Ross said: 'Your mission is urgent and vital. If you fail, it means war. You must not fail.'

The audience was at an end. I left.

I had lunch at a restaurant, alone. I didn't go back to the hotel in case Sadie called; there was a trip I intended to make without her dogging my heels. After dark, I decided, was the time to see Sadie.

Already, I had the feeling of the general

set-up in Marsport, but although that's the capital, it certainly isn't all Mars. And I wanted to get outside to test the feeling there. I hired a runabout to take me to a public airlock. There I saw a man who ran trips outside.

He was Martian, of course, and didn't care for the idea of showing me around. I produced my official papers, and a copy of one of my books.

'I'm an author,' I explained, 'looking for background material for a story.'

I was lucky. This Martian had heard of me.

He'd read one of my books and liked it. That won him over. In the end, he got quite enthusiastic about helping me, after I'd promised to fit him into the story I was writing.

'I'll take you,' he said, 'and no charge. I'll be a pleasure, Mr. Black. Where do you want to go?'

Without batting an eyelid, I said:

'The Vestal uranium mines.'

He looked at me with suspicion in his eyes. Obviously, he was reluctant to take an Earthman to the mines — and that made me all the keener to go. I kept a blank, innocent face and said:

'One of the chief characters in my story is a miner. I don't want to slip up on detail.'

It seemed to satisfy him, for he gave me the usual form to sign, absolving him of all responsibility in case of accident. A trip outside is no picnic.

Mars is largely desert, an utterly desolate world, more like the moon than it is the Earth. The thin air is poisonous and un-breathable. The surface is mainly flat, but it is studded with craters and ravines — twin products of both meteoric and ancient volcanic action. It is covered with a very fine sand, so fine that it is akin to dust. The dust is gathered up by the thin winds, and the resultant dust storms can last for minutes, hours, or even days.

The Martian's name was Jarold and he made his living by driving a caterpillar, running trips outside the colony. He didn't appear half so anti-Terran as some people I'd met in the last twenty-four hours. I speculated on whether this could be due to the fact of his spending so much time away from Marsport.

The caterpillar started off looking like a tank.

It was completely armoured and airtight, and the front windscreen was made of specially toughened glassite that both screened radiation and was resistant to the abrasion of flying dust particles. It had a bulldozer accessory for forcing a path through dust and sand drifts.

I settled into the bucket seat beside the driver, and we set off, passing through the airlock to the outside of the dome. The desert started at once, and our caterpillar ploughed straight into it, sending up plumes of dust.

The Vestal mines were the largest on Mars, also the nearest to the capital. The planet is rich in uranium, which means that a high standard of life is possible by utilizing atomic power; but Uranium can also be used for building atomic bombs and other weapons of terrible destructive power. I wanted to visit the mines to gauge the output of uranium ore; that would be a pointer to whether the

Martians were going in for mass-production of atomic weapons

Theoretically, anyone could visit the mines. In practice, Earthmen were discouraged. The inference was obvious and not very pleasant. It remained to be seen whether I should be allowed to look around.

The caterpillar was making good speed, following an established route that skirted any large craters and boulders. Overhead, tiny ribbons of cloud did nothing to block out the sun, but it was a tiny sun, its light less than half that on Earth. Nonetheless, I knew that the vitiated atmosphere was allowing much of its harmful ultra-violet radiation to bombard the planet. The surface of Mars was a dangerous place to be without the appropriate protection. It never rained, had never rained for thousands, perhaps millions of years.

After a while the driver clicked his tongue and gave a sharp intake of breath.

'What is it?' I asked. 'Trouble?'

'Could be.' He pointed ahead, to our left. 'Look over there.'

I noticed a swirling eddy of yellowish

dust on the horizon. As I watched it grew larger. 'A dust storm?'

'That's right. Let's hope it's just a small one.'

The dust storm grew steadily, and I cringed a little as it began making an eerie scratching sound against the side of our vehicle. Jarold gave me an amused sideways glance.

'It can't penetrate our reinforced armour,' Jarold told me. 'Only thing to worry about is that if it's prolonged enough, it might build up between our treads.' He pressed switches, and a blank screen suddenly glowed into greenish life.

'Radar,' Jarold explained. 'I'm looking for a small ravine or crater where we can lie low till it passes.'

The dust swirled and rattled itself about the caterpillar, completely blocking the view ahead.

'Good — there's a ravine a hundred yards ahead,' Jarold said, studying the radar screen, and changing course slightly to head towards it.

We were lucky. The storm blew itself out within twenty minutes, and we were able to crawl out of the ravine and continue our journey.

We reached Vestal without further incident.

The mines were worked under a huge air-containing dome. We passed through the double airlock and I stepped outside and looked about me. I didn't need to look hard to confirm my worst fears. Uranium ore was being mined and treated at a speed quite out of keeping with any industrial project. The work was going on at such a pace, and under such pressure, that could only be justified by the probability of immediate war. They just could not use all that ore in the natural course of power production. It was obvious I wasn't going to be allowed to probe deeper.

A mining official intercepted me promptly.

'Your papers?' he said. 'What is your business here?'

I established my identity.

'I'm planning a book set on Mars and one of my characters is a uranium miner. I'd like to look around and — '

'Quite impossible.'

His tone was cold. It wasn't openly anti-Earth, but just as definite. The hatred was veiled, but it was there just the same.

I protested mildly: 'But I have permission. I was told I could expect full cooperation — '

'I regret that is impossible.'

He searched for a way out of the impasse. Theoretically, I had authority on my side. Theoretically. I wondered if he thought I'd already seen too much. I didn't like the idea of becoming an interplanetary incident.

He said: 'You must return to Marsport at once. There has been an accident, a leakage of radioactivity. I cannot take responsibility for your safety.'

It was an inspired piece of lying. I pretended to accept his statement at face value.

'Of course. In that case, I will go back now.'

Jarold looked unhappy. He was beginning to realize he'd blundered in bringing me to Vestal at all. We climbed inside the caterpillar and left the dome. Jarold didn't speak to me all the way back.

From my point of view the trip had been a success. I'd tested local feeling outside the capital. It was prejudiced against Earth, a hatred that would soon lead to war. The feeling was veiled, but it was still dangerous. I didn't need to test other colonies; I knew it would be the same right across the planet.

And I'd seen for myself that the Martians were mining Uranium to feed their war machine. That meant I hadn't long to solve the problem. I had to work fast, root out the people behind this war fever and deal with them. But how? I couldn't see any immediate line to take . . . and time was short. I began to feel worried.

At Marsport, I took a runabout to my hotel. I went to my room and let myself in. Then I discovered I wasn't alone. Sadie Lubinski was waiting for me.

4

The man who vanished

Sadie reclined comfortably on the settee. Her green hair was contrasted by a wine-red gown — a strapless, off-the-shoulder affair that was no more substantial than the one I'd seen her in before. Looking at her lying there, slim and shapely, my pulse stirred a fraction. Only a fraction. If I hadn't been wary of her professional intentions, it would have leapt clear off the chart.

'You were going to call me,' she accused. 'Why didn't you?'

I sat down opposite her. I didn't trust myself to get too close. She was digging for information.

'I did. You were out.'

'You could have called back,' she pointed out.

I couldn't evade that one.

I said: 'I went outside. It could have

been dangerous to take you with me —
the desert is no place for a woman.'

She looked at me with reproach in her
eyes.

'You promised to take me along. And I
had such wonderful ideas to help with the
book.'

'It's shaping all right,' I said uneasily. 'I
got an incident while I was outside.' I told
her about the dust storm.

She commented: 'That should make
good reading — dramatized!'

I grinned.

'Maybe I'll dramatize my meeting with
you.'

She lowered her eyes and said, softly:
'You don't have to, Alec. I thought you
knew that.' Her eyes came up again,
steady on me.

My lips dry, I rose to my feet. I crossed
over to the settee and sat beside her. Her
perfume set the blood tingling in my
veins and I silently cursed the fates
that decreed we should be on opposite
sides.

Abruptly, I said: 'Last night, I ran into
an anti-Terran mob. If I hadn't ducked

for cover, you'd be sending me flowers right now.'

She was silent and, for a moment, I thought she was going to cry. She stood up, not looking at me.

'You don't trust me, Alec, I see that now. Because I'm a colonist. I thought that wouldn't matter, between us. I was wrong. My feelings — '

She checked herself. I followed her across the room.

'Yes,' I said. 'Go on. How do you feel about me?'

'It doesn't matter now. I'll leave.'

In the doorway, she paused and turned. 'Are you going back to Earth, Alec?'

'No. I'm staying in Marsport till I've finished my story. I don't scare easily.' She bit her lip.

'It might be better if you did. Just now, Mars is dangerous for Earthmen. It would be best if you returned to your own planet.'

As she went out, I said: 'I'll call you tomorrow.'

Then the door closed and I was alone. I stood in the centre of the room, thinking.

There could be no doubt I'd received a warning — but was it official? Was she acting under orders? Or did Sadie really care what happened to me? I began to realize, uneasily, that it mattered to me whether she cared or not.

I spent the next few minutes searching my room. She might have planted a spymechanism. I found nothing.

The next morning an official message-form lay on my breakfast table. It was short and direct.

You are requested to present yourself for interview with Mr. Oving,
Room No.313, Immigration Authority,
at ten hundred hours.

I didn't like the smell of it at all. A message like that is practically an order. I imagined myself being forcibly deported as an undesirable,

I left the hotel and walked towards the spaceport. Immigration Authority was a tall, white-stone block pushing up towards the dome of Marsport; a severe and efficient-looking building.

I stepped into the hallway and up to the reception desk. A clerk directed me to a row of lift cages set in one wall, and said:

'Third floor.'

The cage was self-operating. I thumbed a button and went up. The third floor corridor was bare and white, like a hospital. I found 313, knocked and went in. The girl behind the desk smiled and said:

'Mr. Black?'

She pressed a switch, murmured into a microphone. She waved me towards an inner room.

'Go right in. Mr. Oving is expecting you.'

I pushed open the door of the inner room and walked in. I closed the door. The room was long and narrow, with a raised platform at one end. A man sat in a large padded chair on the platform, looking down at me.

'Sit down. Mr. Black,' he said.

I sat down, thinking how carefully this had been planned. I was supposed to feel inferior at the end of that long room, seated on a low, hard stool, forced to look up at the man who had sent for me. The stool was so low that my knees stuck up in the air.

Mr. Oving smiled pleasantly. There were purple drapes hanging behind him, a warm light around him. My end of the room was bare, the light colder. It was very subtle.

Oving said: 'I'm glad you came, Mr. Black. I have received a report from the police department — you were fortunate to escape with your life. My congratulations.'

I kept my voice level.

'Thanks.'

Oving was stoutly built, paunchy, with a bald head. His eyes were close-set about a hooked nose, his skin sallow. He had a hanging lower lip and cold, reptilian eyes, and I didn't like the way he leaned forward to look at me, as if I were a specimen on a dissecting table.

He said: 'We are, of course, flattered that such a well-known author as yourself should entertain the idea of writing a story set on our planet — '

Our planet! How deliberately he

51

emphasized the two words. I felt uneasy. Just how much did Oving suspect? After all, I was supposed to be a secret agent . . .

' — but in view of the unsettled conditions here, we think it would be better if you returned to Earth.'

'A few more days would be all I need,' I said.

There was something about his eyes that had an unnerving effect on me. They suggested he had looked on things he did not care to reveal. I let my gaze drop from his face.

'I am reluctant to order you to leave Mars, Mr. Black. I merely suggest that it would be to your advantage. You are in considerable danger while you remain here.'

I said, carefully: 'I shall, of course, take care not to become involved in any trouble with the colonists. My policy is to observe, not to take part in political arguments. In fact, my sympathy is very largely with the Martians in this particular matter.'

Oving let the silence grow into tension before replying.

'It is for you to decide, Mr. Black. It is your life that is threatened, not mine. If you wish to stay on Mars, well . . . if that is your choice, you must stand by the consequences. I simply advise you to leave, at once. While this unrest troubles us, no Earthman is safe in Marsport. Surely you see that? Surely you see that my request is solely motivated by a desire for your welfare?'

I stood up.

'I'll be leaving — soon,' I said.

'Very well.' Oving made a small gesture with his right hand. 'Let us hope you will not leave it too late. Good day, Mr. Black.'

I left, wondering why I had been summoned. It wasn't till I was going down in the lift that I realized just how much impression Oving had made on me.

His personality was overwhelming. He didn't need that trick with the long room, the lighting, and the raised platform. For a moment, I considered whether it had been an attempt to save me from the direct impact of his forceful personality; whether my attention had been taken from the man and made to rest on the setting. No, that was too fantastic. I shrugged off the uneasy feeling that my innermost thoughts had been penetrated by some alien witchcraft. Certainly, Mr. Oving was a very strange man. Again I felt doubts about my ability to handle this job.

Perhaps this was intended as official confirmation of the warning Sadie had given me last night. A threat, diplomatic, but nonetheless real — following my trip to the Vestal uranium mine? I could only ignore it.

It was lunchtime when I returned to the hotel. I ate without tasting the food, then retired to my room. After all, I was supposed to be a writer. I sat at my console and typed out a heading: VENDETTA ON MARS BY ALEC BLACK, CHAPTER ONE. I sat back and thought. I had to be careful not to put anything into the story connected with real events on Mars. This had to be traditional space-adventure. I began:

Without warning, a violet death ray

stabbed the shadows. *Cosmo Scott* ducked, grabbing for his own ray gun. His gun-arm came up with lightning speed and he blasted his would-be killer to atoms. But the space pilot was not alone. Cosmo saw a second figure skulking in the darkness, a huge, scowling fellow with a black beard. Cosmo feinted sideways, firing again. His ray withered the pirate's right arm, and he fell, dying.

Cosmo Scott moved grimly forward and bent over the dying man. His bronzed, handsome face was lined, his jaw set, his blue eyes sparkled.

'Speak up, you swine,' he demanded sternly.

'Who paid you to set this ambush?'

'Curse you, Cosmo Scott,' the pirate gasped with his dying breath. 'It was the Space Hound. He has Miss Evarard a prisoner on Mars!'

A tortured oath fell from Cosmo's lips. The very blood froze in his veins. His lovely Eve in the hands of the Space Hound! He straightened up, his bronzed fists clenched, swearing *revenge if any harm should come to her. He must go to Mars at once. He must save her . . .*

And so on till the end of Chapter One. I rocketed Cosmo to Mars, pitched him into trouble right up to his ears, and left the hotel.

It was evening by the clock, but the scene under the dome of Marsport had changed little. Day-shift workers were strolling the boulevards, looking for entertainment. I joined them. I came to a hall that had the notice outside:

MASS MEETING
MARS FOR THE MARTIANS

I slipped through the open doors and joined the back row of the audience. It was a large hall, circular, with tiers of seats rising from a central speaking dais. The seats were filled and men were standing at the back. No one took any notice of me as I stood in the shadow of an ornamented arch. I listened to the speaker.

' — we will no longer yield to the yoke of Earth's tyranny. We must stand up for our rights, fight for the right to be free. Freedom for ourselves and our children. Freedom to work as we please, to develop the resources of our planet, to live our own lives in our own homes. That is my message to you. Mars for the Martians!'

The wave of applause was nearly deafening. People clapped, cheered, stamped their feet. It was some minutes before the next speaker was able to make himself heard.

'My friends, you have heard our plan for action. I propose to show how this must be effected. It means war — war against Earth! There can be no compromise, no concessions. Either we are our own masters or Earth's slaves. Do not be misled by those who would tell you Terra's aims are peaceful. Our agents report tremendous activity in Earth's war industries. They are recruiting armies, building mighty ships of space-war, stepping up production of atomic bombs and other radioactive weapons. They mean to crush us utterly . . .'

'But we are prepared. Our space fleet is stronger than Earth knows. Our war potential grows daily. Soon we will be ready to strike. And we must strike first. We cannot wait for the enemy to come to us — it would be too late then. We must carry the fight to Terra! We must annihilate our conquerors, lay waste their evil planet, destroy every last vestige of their existence!'

'The day of liberation is near at hand. The torch of freedom is lit — soon it will blaze across space to become a funeral pyre for our oppressors. Never again will Martians acknowledge the omnipotence of Earth. Never again will we cower before the tyrants. Never — never — never! War is a cleansing agent. On the wings of righteous war we will sweep Earthmen from the system forever. People of Mars, I give you a slogan: WAR BEFORE FREEDOM!'

The audience took up the slogan, chanting it, stamping their feet in unison.

'*War before freedom . . . war before freedom . . . war before freedom!*'

This was worse than I'd ever imagined.

This was no amateurish propaganda on the part of a few malcontents, but an organized and highly emotional tirade calculated to build up war fever to such a pitch of intensity that only the action of war could satisfy it. And still I had no lead to the men behind the plot.

It was obviously dangerous for me to remain in the hall, so I started to make my way back to the door. It was then I saw the small man again.

I stood quite still, forgetting even to breathe till a tightness about my chest reminded me. He was twenty feet away, behind the crowd standing at the back of the hall, watching me. I could not fail to recognize him. He wore the same grey suit, a pale-faced man with hard-to-define features. A nonentity, ordinary, inconspicuous.

A quiver of fear travelled through my body. I suppressed it. I forced my legs to walk towards him. Who he was I had no idea. He looked an average Martian — a bit too average. But no Martian has the power to vanish into thin air. I wanted to touch the small man, to assure myself that he really existed. I wanted to get him alone and question him.

I was almost up to him when it happened. Another second and I could have reached out my arm and touched him. *Then he turned and walked through the wall behind him.*

I reached the spot and punched the wall with my fist. The skin was scraped off my knuckles. Pain shot through my hand. The wall was solid the way most walls are. No one could walk through it . . . but the small man had.

I went into the nearest bar and downed a stiff drink. The small man had been watching me. Why? Was he one of those planning to engulf Earth and Mars in war? Surely he could not simply be a Martian agent? I shook my head. There was more to it than that and I had to get to the bottom of the mystery in a hurry. I didn't have long to prevent an interplanetary war.

When I got back to the hotel there was a message waiting. Fisher of the Terran Intelligence wanted to see me in the morning.

5

Pride of race

The morning was the same as any other in Marsport — dry and artificial. Outside the dome, a dust storm had developed. I could hear the rhythmic murmuring of the dust particles on the dome overhead as I walked through the streets.

The sound was barely above the lower limit of human audibility, an incessant whispering, a pattering, a rustling. I was conscious of it, irritable. Martians had got used to the sound and ignored it. I was new and sensitively aware of it. You could pick out the Terrans that morning; they kept glancing up to the roof of the dome.

As I walked, I wondered what Fisher would have to report. Fisher was chief of the Terran Intelligence Service on Mars, temporarily under my orders till this business was cleared up. I'd met him once before and liked him. He was a good agent.

I had plenty of time to make the rendezvous, and let my steps wander from the direct route. But I did not travel haphazardly. My course took me past the three largest armament factories in Marsport. The first specialized in small arms. There was an air of bee-like activity about the place. Men and machines worked with robot precision. There were no slackers.

I strolled on and reached the second factory. Here, delicate mechanisms for the remote control of atomic weapons were manufactured. I glanced in through the windows, taking an idle interest in the work. Mostly women, heads down, hands moving rapidly, intent on their work. I noticed the building had been recently enlarged.

Further on, I came to a plant where metals for the war machine were forged from crude ores. There was tension here, the feeling of men working desperately against time. I didn't need to see a production chart to guess that the red line had long since climbed off the graph paper.

No one stopped me. The factories were legitimate and certainly not on secret work. What frightened me was the volume of output and the tremendous industry everyone showed. These were people who did not doubt they were preparing a war for freedom, that they could win against the might of Earth.

I continued towards my rendezvous. Time was short; shorter, perhaps, than I realized — but there was nothing I could do. No action was possible until I had facts to go on. An agent's job is like that. Slow, tedious, routine. It gave me a sense of frustration. The murmuring of the dust didn't help, either.

I came out on a wide boulevard as the hands of a clock pointed towards eleven hundred hours. Opposite, people sat drinking and talking at tables outside a chromium and plastic fronted bar. Soft music filtered through a screen of exotic blooms, a blend of quiet melody and bright, raucous colour.

I crossed the street. Fisher was there,

waiting. I watched for his signal; he would ignore me if it was dangerous for us to meet. He waved a greeting and I walked to his table and sat down. We ordered drinks.

'How's the new story going?' he asked.

'Fine,' I said.

'Noticed the bookshops? I've been pushing your latest, *Death on Deimos*. It's selling well. Funny how some people still prefer to read actual paper books these days. I handle the production side myself.'

Fisher would attend to details like that; he had a meticulous mind for routine work. We talked idly of books, for the benefit of any casual listener. Fisher was, on the surface, the Mars representative of my publisher — so it was only natural that we should meet. I could have gone to his office, but our conversation might have been tapped. Not because Fisher was suspect, but because he was an Earthman.

In the open, we could talk with a minimum risk of being overheard. We were alone, our table sufficiently apart from the others to ensure privacy. I looked at him and said, critically:

'You're putting on weight.'

Fisher grinned. He was a round barrel of a man with a fat, red face adorned by a ragged bristle of moustache. Anyone less like the conventional picture of a secret agent would be difficult to imagine. He said, pitching his voice lower:

'I've got something for you.'

I refrained from leaning towards him. My voice was controlled at a level just below that which the Martian at the next table could hear. 'Let's have it.'

Fisher said: 'There's a secret war factory, underground. I suspect it is being used to build atomic weapons.'

My skin prickled. This sounded like the real thing.

'Where is it?' I asked.

'You know the early settlement that's being pulled down?' I nodded; I knew that area too well — it was where I'd nearly been lynched by the mob. Fisher continued: 'The entrance is an empty warehouse labelled, Martian Exports. I've checked in a number of cargoes of uranium ore. The lorries came back empty. There's nothing on the surface, so there must be a tunnel underground.'

'Anything else?'

'The lorries only go in and out at night,' Fisher said. 'We must get a man in there and find out exactly what is going on.'

I nodded; that much was obvious — but how was it to be done? The Martians would take stringent precautions to prevent spies getting through, and any Terran caught there would be dealt with on the spot. And I didn't have the faculty for disappearing into thin air . . .

Abruptly, I said: 'Have you seen anything of a small man in a grey suit who makes a habit of walking through walls?'

Fisher gave me an odd look. 'Is that meant to be funny?' he said.

I returned to the problem of the factory. I could have given Fisher the job of detailing a man to risk his life by trying to penetrate this underground factory; that would have been the easy way out.

But I like to sleep at night and that can be difficult after you've ordered a man to his death. A commander should be prepared to take the first risk.

I said: 'I'll go myself. Tonight.'

Fisher said, unnecessarily: 'It's dangerous. Perhaps you'd like assistance?'

I shook my head.

'No, I'll go alone. One man stands less chance of detection than two. If you've a man watching the place, take him off. I want a clear field — keep your men well away from that area for twenty-four hours.'

'And after that?'

'After that,' I said, 'you'll be in charge. Take whatever action you think necessary.'

He stood up to leave. We didn't shake hands.

He said, 'Good luck with the book,' and turned and walked off. He was soon lost in the crowd.

I sat a while longer, took another drink. No one followed Fisher. I might see him again — I might not. It depended on whether my luck held tonight; he knew that, and his last remark had nothing to do with my literary work.

Life tasted pleasant for a moment. The small pleasures were highlighted, ordinary sensations heightened. The air smelled sweeter, colours looked brighter. Tomorrow, none of this might exist for me . . .

I left the table and sauntered easily along the boulevard. From time to time, I stopped, gazed into a shop window. The reflection told me I had no follower. Our meeting appeared to have gone unnoticed by those who would be most interested. That was some small relief.

I headed back for the hotel. There was the usual noise of traffic, of people bustling by, fragments of conversation. Then it subtly changed. There was an uncanny silence; or, rather, the cessation of some particular sound I had taken for granted. The noise of traffic and people went on undisturbed. For a moment I stood still, perturbed by a feeling of something missing; then I realized what had happened.

The dust storm had passed. The background murmuring of the dust on the roof of the city switched off as suddenly as an electric current at the turn of a switch. The change was startling. I think it is the first time I was ever conscious of the absence of sound.

I reached my hotel and ate a light lunch before returning to my console and *Vendetta on Mars*. I typed a fresh heading and started writing Chapter Two:

Cosmo Scott faced a hideous death. Trapped in the hidden lair of the Space Hound, in the vast Martian cave, he stood with his hands bound at his back while the lovely Eve Evarard advanced towards him, a glittering knife in her hand.

'Eve,' he said hoarsely, 'stop! Wake up!'

The drugged girl advanced, helpless to prevent herself carrying out the Space Hound's command.

The knife she held was poisoned — one scratch and Cosmo would die at the hands of the girl he loved.

The Space Hound laughed, a sinister sound that echoed eerily through Cosmo's prison.

'A fitting death,' the pirate chief gloated.

'No more shall Cosmo Scott trouble me. Strike, girl, strike!'

'No,' gasped Cosmo. 'Eve — no!'

Eve Evarard did not stop. Her eyes glazed, her very brain under the Space Hound's control, she lifted the poisoned knife to plunge it straight into Cosmo Scott's heart . . .

I pushed back my chair, rose disconsolately. I couldn't concentrate. I might be facing a 'hideous' death myself very shortly and Cosmo Scott's dilemma seemed unimportant.

I paced the room, thinking. What did I hope to achieve tonight? At best, I could hope to wreck part of the plant and push back the immediate threat of war for a little time. My job was not to spy on secret armament factories. My job was to expose and ruin the men behind the plot — and that was far more difficult. I might be risking my life to no purpose; yet I had to go through with it. There might be the lead I wanted, hidden in the underground factory.

I remembered Sadie — and thought of dying without seeing her again. The thought was unbearable. I used the visiphone to call her number. The screen glowed. I saw her, heard her voice.

'Alec, you do look odd! Is something the matter?'

I said: 'Sadie, I've got to see you. Right away. Will you come here or shall I meet you somewhere?'

She paused, hesitating before replying, and I took a good look at her. She was lovely.

Caution edged her voice. 'What do you want to see me about?'

'You know why,' I said. 'I don't have to put it into words for you. I must see you again.'

She hesitated so long I thought she was going to turn me down. Then she said:

'Stay there. I'll come over, in about fifteen minutes.'

I broke the connection and pushed my laptop into a corner. I punched the cushions on the settee, ordered a bottle of wine to be sent up. A pulse beat inside my head. This might be the last time I'd see

Sadie, our last few hours together.

The wine arrived. I tipped the waiter lavishly; very likely I'd have no use for money in a short while. I fretted impatiently, looking at my watch every thirty seconds. The hands crawled round. Once, I thought the mechanism had stopped. I shook the watch, held it to my ear, listening to the rhythmic ticking. I was sweating a little.

This is crazy, I told myself. She's a Martian agent, you can't expect her to care about you. You can't explain anything.

The pulse in my head beat faster. Your last chance, it said. Tomorrow is eternity, a dark void, nothing. Only this moment exists. Tell her before it's too late.

The doorbell buzzed. I knocked my shin on a chair getting to the door. I opened it and she was there. Her calmness quieted my racing nerves,

'You were going to call me yesterday,' she said, coming in.

I closed the door.

'I know. I was busy on my story.'

I took her wrap. She was wearing the

red, off-the-shoulder gown again. I held her close while I kissed her.

'How's it going?' she asked.

'I got stuck in chapter two — that's when I called you.'

She sat on the settee, pushed back a stray curl of green hair. She patted the cushions at her side, looking at me with grave, copper eyes. I poured the wine and handed her a glass.

'What shall we drink to?' she asked. 'Success with your book?'

I shook my head.

'No, not that. Drink to — tonight . . . '

There was the slightest pause before her red lips curved in a smile.

'Very well.' Her tone was gentle, comforting. How much did she guess? 'To — tonight!'

Our glasses touched. I drained mine, but Sadie sipped hers slowly. We sat in silence for a while. I was content to sit and look at her, thinking how lovely she was. Then a nagging doubt started at the back of my mind. She was a spy set to watch me. I couldn't trust her. She'd only come to draw me out, to learn what I had discovered. She was dangerous. I must be careful —

Tomorrow I might be dead.

Sadie finished her drink and set down the glass. Her eyes had a great sadness in them.

I took her in my arms and kissed her. Her arms wound about my neck and we clung together. We both knew this meant something; we weren't playing now. Her cheek was moist against mine.

'Sadie,' I whispered. 'I love you, love you, darling.'

'Don't — '

She pushed me away, suddenly, urgently. I saw that she was crying. It hurt to see her cry.

'Sadie,' I said, 'darling!'

She stood up, keeping away from me. Her face worked through changing expressions; sadness, love, anger, hatred — it was all there. Her voice quivered.

'Leave me alone, Alec. I'm ashamed of myself. I hate you, hate you, hate you!'

'That's not true,' I said quietly. 'You know it isn't.'

'It is!' She flared up, angrily. 'I hate you

because you're an Earth spy taking advantage of me. I hate all Earthmen. There can be no love between us, only hatred. Your government is preparing to make war on Mars — don't deny it! — and you were sent here to spy. You thought you could make love to me and force me to reveal our secrets. Well, you've failed. I despise and hate you. You're mean, and low, and — oh, leave me alone!'

Her face was white and tear-stained. Her hands were clenched into tiny fists. Her eyes blazed.

'I'm proud of being Martian, Alec. You wouldn't understand that. All you think of is power and conquest and war; that's all any Terran thinks of. Making love to me is just another trick in the plan for subduing Mars. It won't work, Alec. We're a proud race. I won't become a pawn to be sacrificed to your God of War.'

She was like a wild cat, spitting, her claws out.

'I'm leaving for good now. You won't see me again. I hate you. I hope you drop dead!'

She ran out of the room, slamming the door.

I sat down. I felt weak, completely washed out. Sadie was gone and I cursed the chief for handing me this job. I had no further interest in living. She meant that much.

A clock chimed, reminding me of the time. It was growing late — and still I had a job to do. I set about making my preparations — for the night's work.

6

Spies can be lonely

Martian Exports was easily found. I lay in shadow atop the wall of an adjacent building, watching the empty warehouse Fisher had described. There was a high wall surrounding a bleak-looking yard, a shed with half the roof missing and the doors hanging off. It was palpably derelict. I saw no sign of life. There was no light or movement from the shadows far back under what was left of the roof.

I kept still and silent and waited. Presently, from the direction of the weakly-lit streets over to my left, came the sound of a motor. The sound increased in volume and headlamps swung across the wall below me. A wagon moved smoothly past, into the yard. It was a large wagon, with its cargo concealed by a hood and nothing about it to arouse suspicion.

As I watched, the wagon drove inside

the shed — and vanished. I could hear the sound of the motor fading in the distance. So Fisher was right about the tunnel. I waited for the next wagon to arrive, my course of action planned, my mind made up.

I did not have long to wait. The deep throb of an engine carried to my ears. The beam of a headlamp lit the wall — then the top of the wagon was directly beneath me. I jumped; and hit the plastic hood with my feet and sprawled flat, face down, clutching at rib projections to hold on. The wagon entered the shed and kept going.

The headlamp showed a curving arch of roof that came down sharply as the tunnel sloped into the ground. There was very little clearance between the top of the wagon and the roof; obviously, the tunnel had been specially constructed to take vehicles of a certain size. I hoped the ground remained level; if the wagon bounced, I was in danger of being crushed against the arch of the tunnel.

We travelled downwards for some distance, the tunnel swinging in a gentle curve. There came a halt. Men appeared, armed and uniformed. The driver showed his pass. The cargo was inspected. I held my breath and prayed that the guards would not think of looking on top of the hood. My luck held. The driver was waved on.

The wagon continued its journey down the tunnel. It hit me all at once that I was right over a load of radioactive uranium, and again I got scared. I hoped the stuff was well-shielded.

The journey became monotonous. There was the never-ending arch of the tunnel, the bright beam of the headlamp, the muffled roar of the engine. The tunnel still sloped down at an angle, boring deeper beneath the surface of the planet. I wondered if our destination lay below one of the factories I had visited that morning.

My muscles began to ache from the strain of hanging on to the smooth surface of the wagon's hood. My neck had a crick in it. I thought of Sadie and how unlikely it was that I'd see her again, and that gave me an empty feeling. It isn't nice to feel you are completely alone in a nightmare world — and that's how it seemed to me.

I imagined myself being carried along on the top of the wagon forever, driving endlessly through an eternal tunnel into darkness. On and on, seeing no one, speaking to no one, getting nowhere. There was infinite, time and infinite space — and infinite loneliness. It was like being suspended over an abyss, on the point of falling, but never quite falling. Suspended, floating through a dream from which there can be no awakening.

Sadie was a fever in my blood. Not to be with her was the incarnation of all loneliness. That her love for me should turn to hatred because she believed I had used her in the game of war was a torment. The agony of knowing I had lost her was worse.

I was glad when the long drive ended and the wagon drew up before closed steel gates. The check was superficial; the guards here assumed that the men at the first checkpoint had done their work. Again, no one thought to look on top of the hood. The gates slid noiselessly open. The wagon passed through. The doors closed again.

I had the nervous feeling that freedom had gone forever, an excitement at penetrating the secret underground factory. Involuntarily, the tip of my tongue licked at the capsule contained within the hollow tooth in my mouth. I was careful not to crush it — later, in an emergency, I might have need of it.

There was no shadow to hide me now. I was in a world of bare concrete and harsh floodlighting. The roof was high overhead and anyone looking down from the windows in the buildings that rose on either side could hardly fail to see me. The wagon roared up a wide roadway to its unloading point.

Men in white coats gathered about the wagon.

One had a geiger counter; it tripped mechanically, slowly. They began to unload the cargo of small lead containers, carrying them into a storeroom,

They were very intent on their business.

I took advantage of their preoccupation and dropped lightly to the ground on the far side of the wagon. I walked away from the store shed, keeping the wagon between myself and their line of vision. The road was broad and empty, lined with buildings from which came the high-pitched hum of machinery. There was no one to see me; on the other hand, alone on that flat stretch of concrete, I should immediately become an object for suspicion if a chance eye fell on me.

I decided that what I wanted was a white coat. The simplest disguise is always the best, and, with a white coat over my suit, I should be taken for one of the workers at first glance. And no one was going to look for an Earthman in this secret place.

The doorway of the nearest building bore the plaque:

ACTIVE LABORATORY

I went inside. There was a hallway with cubicles and a shower, coats hanging in a row. I put on one of the white coats and helped myself to a geiger counter. It was a near certainty that in an atomic plant there would be monitors checking for leakage of radioactivity. My disguise was complete.

I walked along a corridor to a door with a red light outside. I opened the door and caught a glimpse of masked workers before a uranium pile. My counter rattled like a machine-gun. I backed out hurriedly.

I left the active building and snooped around, passing several Martians without exciting comment. In my disguise, they took me for one of themselves. In one department I saw warheads being loaded with atomic bombs; in another, men built the remote-control rockets, which would carry death across space. I saw chemists preparing radioactive dusts and gases that would lay barren the ground on which they fell.

The underground factory was more extensive than I'd thought possible. It employed thousands, and the weapons were the most terrible man could conceive. I was badly scared. There could not be the least doubt about the Martians planning an all-out war against Earth, and if I'd been a little sceptical about their power to successfully combat Terran might, my scepticism vanished as I moved from building to building.

Earth would win in the end, of course, but millions would die in the catastrophe. The Mars colony would be annihilated, the work of three generations wasted. It would all have to be done over again.

And, on Earth, vast areas of land would be uninhabitable, food supplies poisoned by radioactivity, more millions would die of plague from the litter of unburied corpses — too many to bury or cremate while a war had to be fought.

My blood boiled at the thought. War was futile, criminally wasteful. Inevitably, the victor lost almost as much as the defeated. I was wasting time. My job was to reach the men behind this plot and expose them; to show the Martians how they had been misled.

I walked on and came to a large building with the notice:

ADMINISTRATION

Here, if anywhere, I would find the men I sought, the proof I wanted to set before the people. I pushed open the door and went in. I was more conspicuous now. No one here wore a white coat, and a geiger counter was unnecessary. But to shed my disguise would be even more dangerous. I told myself that my luck would hold . . .

It didn't. In the hallway, two men were talking. One looked at me, frowning.

'What do you want here?' he said.

I tried to think out a suitable reply. My efforts were wasted. The second man studied me closely. His breath hissed in sudden intake.

'Earthman!'

He lunged for me and I threw the counter at him. He had to use both hands to catch it. I kicked his ankles from under him and threw a punch at his jaw as he fell. But the first man had time to raise the alarm.

Guards came running down a corridor as I turned for the door. A hand caught at the sleeve of my coat. I let him keep it, slipping out of the coat like an eel and running hard. It was foolish to run — even if I broke away. I couldn't get back to the surface now the alarm had been given. But I didn't stop to think about that.

I was in the open, haring along a wide concrete roadway, looking for cover. Men ran after me, shouting. I expected a shot in the back before I reached the first corner, but no one fired. Orders, I thought — they wanted me alive. I ran faster. There are worse things than being shot.

My luck was out. Round the corner, I ran into trouble. Three men had just come out of a doorway. They heard the shouting, saw me, and moved right across my path. I hit the first one between the eyes, tackled the next man low. Something hit the back of my head, and I stumbled. The others reached me and, immediately, I was at the bottom of a heap of struggling bodies.

I rolled over on my back, kicking out. One man doubled up as my feet landed in his stomach. Another dropped as my fist found his solar plexus. Two men fell across my legs, pinning me to the ground. Others hung onto my arms. A rain of blows knocked me half-dizzy. Even then I did not use the capsule in my hollow tooth.

Breathless, my body aching, I was dragged upright and my hands lashed together. Some of the Martians, those I had hurt, were cursing, staring sullenly at me. I had an idea the only reason I wasn't killed on the spot was because some higher-up had given orders to take me alive. Strong hands held me, supporting me as I was forced, half-stumbling, back to the administration block.

The man I was taken to had thin lips and very penetrating eyes; his dress was less gaudy than that of most Martians. He had the look of a man with authority. He took a good look at me, obviously mentally comparing me with detailed information he had received.

'Mr. Black, isn't it?' he said. 'Would you mind telling me just how you got here?'

His tone of voice was quite polite. But

that didn't fool me; I was in a bad spot, and knew it. Ross would disown me. A spy has no friends when he's caught.

'It would be better,' he said, 'if you answered my question, Mr. Black. If you co-operate, I can guarantee that your death will be both swift and painless. The alternative will be less pleasant.'

It was not a speech calculated to arouse any enthusiasm in me. I decided on a routine bluff.

I said: 'I am Alexander Black, a Terran and a well-known author. If anything should happen to me, the Martian government would have to answer some awkward questions. I demand immediate release.'

He didn't speak to me again. He gave orders to his men.

'Get the car out. Lingstrom will want to deal with him personally.'

I knew that name. Lingstrom was head of the Martian Intelligence Service. It seemed I rated pretty high in the scheme of things. Perhaps I'd stumbled across something really important, without realizing the full implications — or perhaps they just thought I had. We waited for the car to arrive.

The car was large and roomy, with blacked-out windows. I sat with my back to the driver, unable to see where we went. There was an armed guard on each side of me, and the man with the thin lips sat opposite. The car moved off. I guessed we were going back along the tunnel, the way I had come.

My questioner spoke again:

'It would be in the interests of your personal comfort if you made up your mind to answer our questions, Mr. Black. Just how did you get past the guards? And how much have you found out about our activities?'

I ignored him. If I could mystify them, I would live a while longer, long enough, perhaps, to make an attempt at escape. We travelled in silence after that.

The car travelled much faster than the wagon that had brought me underground. I thought we must be getting near the surface again. The thin-lipped man thought so, too. He brought a dark hood from his pocket and pushed my head into it; the hood fastened round my neck and I couldn't see a thing. Obviously they were taking no chances on my recognizing the route above ground.

My face began to sweat and I had difficulty in breathing. I could hear my heart beating and I gasped for air. The minutes dragged by. I hoped we should get wherever we were going before I died from suffocation; it got so bad inside the hood that I had to concentrate on breathing.

When the car stopped, I was dragged out and made to walk a short distance. The floor started to press against my feet, and I guessed we were going up in a lift. I still couldn't see anything and my lungs were fluttering like a pair of broken-down bellows. I walked again till I was jerked to a standstill. The dark hood was removed from my head.

My eyes were watering so badly I didn't see much of the room or its occupants for some minutes. I gulped down air, feeling like a man who has been under water too long. My pulse rate steadied as my lungs got back to normal working, and I began to take an interest in my surroundings.

It was a large room, with curtains across the windows. There were three men besides myself. The guard, who stood directly behind me, his gun levelled at my back; Mr. Oving, of Immigration Authority; and Lingstrom. Oving was a surprise; he must be an important man in the set-up — maybe I'd been called to his office for him to look me over.

I gave my attention to Lingstrom. He was thin, a dapper man with a tuft of beard trimmed to a point. His eyes stared at me in an uncompromising way; they looked like eyes that could go on staring forever, without so much as a blink.

Oving said: 'It's Black, all right.'

I gave him a glance. He was still fat and bald, with reptilian eyes either side of a hooked nose.

Lingstrom said: 'You are going to die, Mr. Black, wake up your mind to that. We know you are an Earth spy. You will tell us what you have learnt first. Refuse, and we shall use pressure.'

He spoke in a flat, emotionless voice; my life meant nothing to him, less than nothing. I licked my lips because they were suddenly dry. I could feel my heart beating again.

I said: 'I've nothing to tell.'

'Very well.'

Lingstrom was still staring at me, hard. Then I felt the strange sensation of something alien crawling about inside my head. It was uncanny, frightening, almost obscene. I panicked; but could not move. It seemed my muscles were paralysed; my thoughts raced crazily, protesting against this incredible invasion of my mind. My reason said it couldn't happen — but there was that crawling, loathsome thing inside my brain, probing deeper with each second. It was as if someone turned over my brain cells like the pages of a book.

Lingstrom was a telepath. And he was reading my mind . . . I tried to block my thoughts. Useless. I recited pieces of nonsense rhyme to myself. That bothered him, but not much. I thought of Sadie — and he recoiled sharply. Something in Lingstrom's makeup was revolted by the way I thought about Sadie. I kept my mind on her. The alien thing in my head went away and I could move again.

Lingstrom said: 'Prepare the serum. We must drug him before I can get to the truth.'

Oving brought out a hypodermic syringe and began to fill the cylinder with a translucent red liquid.

I was staring at Lingstrom, petrified. I couldn't believe that any Martian had the power to do what he had just done to me. I realized I was up against something bigger than I'd ever dreamed — that, at last, I had penetrated to the men behind the plot to plunge Earth and Mars into war.

7

Hideaway

With that realization, I felt the need for immediate action. If I delayed longer, my death was assured. I had to escape from that room. Oving had almost finished filling the hypodermic. Lingstrom stared at me, unspeaking. The single guard kept his gun trained on me.

The guard was the first difficulty. I had to get his gun before I could do anything. I tested the cords binding my wrists; they were tight, but not too strong — I might break them given time to work. And, fortunately, my hands were tied in front of me so that I could see what I was doing.

Oving said: 'Ready. Shall I give it to him now?'

Lingstrom nodded, wagging his tuft of beard.

Oving came toward me, the hypodermic in his hand, ready for the injection. It had to be now . . .

Gently, I used my tongue to lift the capsule from its resting place in the hollow tooth. My jaws came together, crushing it. Fluid ran into my mouth. I swallowed.

I could feel the stuff working, taking effect, but I needed seconds before I got maximum benefit from it. I said:

'Wait. I'll talk. I'll tell you what you want to know.'

Oving hesitated, the light catching his bald head, his lower lip hanging in shadow. Lingstrom snapped:

'Take no notice — he's playing for time. Give him the serum.'

I stepped back a couple of paces, watching distances. The gun in the guard's hand. Oving with his hypodermic. Lingstrom. The door. I rejected the door — it was certain there'd be more guards outside. It would have to be the window. Curtains blocked my view beyond the window; I'd have to take a chance on the drop.

I tried my hands again. The cord gave a little — it would break all right. I didn't know what was in the capsule but I knew how it worked. Earth's chemists had evolved a quick-acting stimulant that released energy direct into the blood stream. The effect of the stimulant lasted only a few minutes, but, during that time. I would have greater strength and speed of reflex.

My brain was ice-cool, my awareness heightened. It seemed as if action in the room slowed down. I was living faster. I had to wait for Oving to approach.

Then I acted. The muscles of my arms strained and the cord snapped like rotting thread. I hit Oving in the belly. He took a long time to drop. By then I had reached the guard. He didn't have a chance to fire, so fast was I travelling. I ripped the gun from his hand and clubbed him with it. Lingstrom was moving, slowly, towards me. His mind reached out . . . I thought of Sadie.

The curtains hampered me as I went through the window. I used them to save myself from cuts as I smashed the glass. I looked down. The drop was more than I'd thought, but there was no turning back now — my incredibly fast reflexes should help. Behind me, Oving had just reached the floor. Lingstrom was shouting, and his words seemed drawn out through a long tube. The door was opening, slowly, I saw guards beyond.

I jumped, feeling an exhilaration at my new powers. I was enjoying the thrill of physical danger. Two floors down, I caught at a window ledge. It was absurdly simple. The ledge seemed to float up to my fingers. I used it to break my fall, then dropped again. I let my legs double under me as I hit the ground.

I rested in the shadow of the wall, my senses returning to normal. The effect of the stimulant wore off very quickly, but it had given me the help I needed. I passed a silent vote of thanks to the backroom boys in Earth's laboratories.

Someone was shouting. I saw guards coming, guns in their hands. I broke cover and ran for my life.

Fortunately there were no ill effects from using the stimulant, for I had only my natural resources to rely on now. I turned the corner and crossed the street. I was in a residential suburb of Marsport and there were few people about. But the lighting was too good; there was nowhere to hide. I had to keep running.

A shot echoed behind me. I jumped the fence of a house and made across the garden, heading for the avenue beyond. It seemed I had spent most of my time on Mars running, and I was getting tired of it. There was a wall; I scrambled over it and dropped to the ground on the far side. My luck was still bad. A uniformed policeman patrolled the street; he shouted: 'Stop! Hi, you — Earthman — stop!'

I dodged round him and ran down a side street. There were too many people looking at me. One man crossed to intercept me. I threw a fist at his jaw and swerved past. There were metal gates open, green grass with children playing. I turned into the park and raced by a fountain where coloured water sprayed about a crystal nymph. A siren whined as a runabout drew up outside the gates; armed men tumbled out, chasing me.

My legs were beginning to ache; my heart pounded. My lungs gasped for air. I couldn't hold the pace much longer. A shot whistled past me, too close for comfort. I put my head down and ran faster,

The park was contained within a high wall. I came upon it behind a row of tall shrubs bearing exotic flowers. I made a flying leap, swung myself over the wall and dropped flat on the other side. I stood a moment, leaning against the wall, panting, getting my breath.

The sound of sirens alarmed me. Wailing echoes floated across the pack. Soon I would be surrounded and taken. The distant roar of a shouting crowd came to me, threatening, urgent. I was desperate. I had to find somewhere to hide — and soon.

Mars was no longer safe for me. Even if I eluded my pursuers, a sharp watch would be kept for me. No longer could I roam at freedom. I should have to stay under cover till I got the chance to leave Marsport. I cursed myself bitterly; my failure might set off the war earlier — and that was what I was supposed to prevent. Somehow, I had to get a message through to the chief, warning him.

Lingstrom had been quick to throw a cordon round the area. I found men waiting for me at the end of the street. I ducked as gunshots came my way. I doubled back and took another turning. Behind me, the volume of shouting increased. Not long now, I thought . . . *this was the end.*

The pack gained on me. I was tiring fast. Only the sheer desperation of my situation kept me going; I was running — quite literally — for my life! Another close shot warned me I could not relax for an instant. It seemed I had been running all my life. Surely this was a nightmare from which I must awaken? Run . . . run . . . run . . .

A runabout came from an intersection, slowing down as it approached me. It was not a police car. I made for it, thinking to take the driver by surprise and steal the car for a getaway. The rear door slid open as the runabout came alongside, and a quiet voice said:

'Get in, Mr. Black. I'll take you out of this.'

I didn't stop to argue. I jumped in the back. The door slid shut and the car accelerated. I had a blurred vision of buildings moving past the window at high speed; my driver took a zigzag course through side streets to throw off pursuit. For the moment I was safe.

I lay back in the pneumatic seat, getting my breath. Then I sat up and took an interest in the man who had saved me. I received a shock. I saw a small man in a grey suit, a man with very ordinary, hard-to-define features. I felt as if someone had emptied a bucket of ice water over my head. I sat, paralysed. This was the man who had disappeared into thin air, the man who had walked through a stone wall.

I heard my voice croak: 'Who are you?'

He replied, evenly: 'A friend, Mr. Black. Trust me. I will explain the things that puzzle you, later.'

He used the most ordinary voice I have ever heard. I looked at him, half-scared he would vanish again, leaving me inside a driverless car moving at high speed. I relaxed in the back seat, closed my eyes and counted to ten. When I opened them again, the small man was still at the wheel, handling the runabout like an expert.

We shook off pursuit and arrived at a blind alley lined on each side with private garages. The man turned the car towards one of the garages; the doors opened automatically and we passed inside, The doors closed. It was dark. After a few seconds, a soft light glowed, showing the garage to be quite bare of fittings.

The small man got out, and I followed him. At the back of the garage, he touched the wall and a panel slid open. There was a lift shaft dropping into the ground. I looked at my rescuer with admiration; he certainly had everything on tap.

'Follow me,' he said. 'There is nothing to fear. I shall take you to a secret hideaway where you will be safe from our enemies.'

Our enemies! So the small man was on my side against Lingstrom. I followed him into the lift. The panel closed and we sank into the ground.

'Who are you?' I asked again.

He smiled gently.

'You may call me Yzz-Five, Mr. Black.'

I stared.

'What's that? A code word?'

'A code word, a name, a label. Does it matter?'

The lift reached the bottom of the shaft. I don't quite know what I expected to find; I hadn't really thought about it. What I saw was a large room littered with equipment that I took to be scientific, but which was completely strange to me. I could find no meaning in any of the odd-looking machinery

'Sit down, Mr. Black,' said Yzz-Five. 'I shall not be long.'

'You're not leaving me here?' I said, in alarm. 'I'm grateful to you, but I've a job to do. Can you put me in touch with the Terran Embassy?'

He repeated, 'Sit down,' and pointed to a chair — a chair that, a few moments before, I would have sworn did not exist. I touched it gingerly; it was solid. I sat down.

'I am not leaving you,' Yzz-Five assured

me. 'But I have one small thing to do before we can talk. I suggest that you rest yourself for what is to come.'

I didn't like the sound of that. I said:

'There's nothing to stop me walking out of here.'

'Isn't there, Mr. Black?'

'No,' I said, and looked for the door.

There wasn't one. No door, no window, nothing. I was in a stone cell, below ground; the walls were solid with no apparent way out. The lighting seemed to be in the air itself, a soft radiance bathing everything in the room. The obvious lack of an exit shook me. Logic said I had come into this room, so there must be a way out — but my eyes couldn't find it.

I turned to Yzz-Five, and said: 'This is no time to play tricks, Tell me what you know about Lingstrom.'

He was stooping over one of the machines, a curious affair, with glittering star-shaped paper-thin wafers of metal, a vision screen, and a box of controls. He was intent on whatever it was he was doing and ignored me. I didn't like the way he treated me as if I were of no importance. I took a step towards him, intending to show him I wasn't completely without willpower of my own.

I only took two steps. I stopped — because I couldn't get any further. It was as if I hit a wall of invisible and unbreakable glass. There was a barrier between us. Without looking up, Yzz-Five said: 'Please keep still, Mr. Black. This is a delicate operation.'

I watched over his shoulder, looking at the screen — and got another shock. I saw Sadie Lubinski. She was indoors, pacing a room, worried. I liked to think she was worried over me. She had on a new outfit, shorts with a loose-fitting blouse. She looked even lovelier. Then it happened.

One moment, she was pacing that distant room . . . Yzz-Five moved a switch . . . *and Sadie walked through the stone wall, into our underground hideaway.*

I stared, incredulous. A prickly feeling moved up my spine; reason said this couldn't be. I saw an expression of bewilderment cross her face. She looked completely dazed; and the suspicion that she and the small man might have been working together left me. I remembered Yzz-Five' s words: 'I have one small thing to do.' I took a deep breath; materializing a person through solid stone was no small thing in my book.

Sadie recovered her senses quickly. She looked round, saw me, and jumped to the wrong conclusion. Her copper eyes sparked angrily.

'Alec! Is this some new trick? You won't get anything out of me — Earth spy!'

'Don't blame me,' I said, 'but it's nice to see you again.' I performed a polite introduction. 'Sadie Lubinski — Yzz-Five.'

The small man bowed slightly.

'I know Miss Lubinski,' he said. 'I have been watching you both for some time. You have a strange affinity for each other.'

'Strange?' I echoed, and looked at Sadie. 'What's strange about it? She's beautiful — and I love her.'

Yzz-Five did not pursue the point. He said: 'It is time for you to learn the truth, and, for that reason, I have brought you here. Remember, there is nothing to fear. I am your friend. It is because you are a man of Earth and a woman of Mars, and there exists this affinity between you, that you have been selected — that, and the fact you are secret agents for your two planets.'

Sadie ignored me. She seemed to have forgotten that the small man had just brought her through a solid wall; she showed no fear when she turned on him. 'Just who are you? And what do you think you're doing? And how did I get here?'

'And how do you perform your vanishing trick? What do you know about Lingstrom?' I added.

Yzz-Five smiled, shaking his head.

'It is not I who will answer your questions. I am going to send you on a journey, and, at the end of it, you will know what you need to know.'

My skin had a sudden attack of goose pimples; somehow, I didn't like his use of the word 'send'.

Sadie said, irrelevantly: 'I'm not dressed for going places.'

Yzz-Five busied himself with another piece of the fantastic apparatus littering the room. It had a large metal cabinet from which an assortment of cables and helices led off; the interlacing spirals and mesh of wires suggested mathematics in three dimensions. The contrast between his ordinariness and these other-worldly machines was frightening.

I took a step nearer, and again came up against that invisible barrier.

Yzz-Five said: 'You must wait, Mr. Black. Do not try to interfere. I have certain preparations to make, and time is short. We have so little time left to avoid the war between your planet and Mars.'

That comforted me a little. At least Yzz-Five and I had the same objective. I did not doubt his word — he had an air about him that suggested he was incapable of telling a lie.

Sadie also hit the glass wall . . . *only it wasn't glass.*

Yzz-Five said: 'You must realize I am a telepath and have powers you do not possess. The barrier I have built between us is a barrier of thought; you cannot break it whatever you do. Please wait, and believe that I mean you no harm.'

Yzz-Five was a telepath — Lingstrom was a telepath. What was the connection between them? I warned the small man: 'Sadie is working for Lingstrom.'

He replied. 'You are wrong, Mr. Black.'

It did not take him many minutes to finish the adjustments he was making to the machine. He opened the door of the cabinet, turned a switch, and stood back. The helices began to vibrate; a steady hum of power came from somewhere in the heart of the coiled cables.

Yzz-Five said: 'All is ready. Take Miss Lubinski's hand, Mr. Black, and step into the cabinet. At the other end, you will learn the answers to the questions that puzzle you. Fear nothing.'

There didn't seem anything else to do. I looked at Sadie. She held out her hand and I took it. Together, we walked into the cabinet between the glowing helices. Suddenly, there was utter darkness.

8

Shock treatment

The darkness lasted. I was conscious only of the pressure of Sadie's hand on mine. It was knowing she was beside me that quelled the panic which rose in me. I said something, but there was no sound. The darkness remained silent, completely silent, without even those small sounds we normally take for granted. The effect was uncanny.

I had no idea of time passing, but, after a while, a faint light showed. It was a diffused light, with no beginning and no end. I looked about me. Sadie was there, her face pale and taut, her hand gripping mine — that was the only material force I felt during our incredible journey. There was nothing under my feet. We existed in a void, an emptiness of light.

I spoke again, and, again there came no

sound. That indicated a lack of atmosphere. But I was still alive, still breathing. Or was I? I tried to detect my breathing, and failed. Was this death? No it couldn't be — not with Sadie beside me, holding my hand. I held on to her as if she were a lifebelt and I a drowning man. She represented sanity in a world gone mad,

I began to see things then. Strange sights floated before my eyes. Worlds — peopled — cities and seas and ships. Images moved past me like scenes from an oddly immaterial Tri-D film — images that changed and changed again, showing new scenes from planets I had never dreamed existed. Or did they exist? Perhaps this was no more than a dream . . .

The void extended to infinity. There was no land under my feet, no air to breathe, and yet I lived. It was beyond comprehension, timeless, an experience to marvel at. The kaleidoscope of changing worlds flashed by, real yet immaterial, there before my eyes, yet unbelievable, The planets swam past, bathed in that diffused light, one after another, coming and going in endless procession. I watched and wondered and felt Sadie grip my hand tighter.

I imagined a giant's hand turning the pages of creation, showing all that had been and all that was to come. I thought of a spaceship cutting through a cross-section of the universe at a speed faster than light. The kaleidoscope went on; world upon world showed for a brief interval before being replaced by the next in line. I saw alien peoples and cities . . . and then it ended.

There was darkness again, and ground under my feet, tiny sounds and smells. Sadie nestled close to me and I put my arm around her. It wasn't quite dark. My eyes got used to the twilight and I began to perceive the dim outline of the countryside, rolling dunes, barren; desolate. I kicked at the ground; powdery soil sprayed up. We seemed to be in the middle of a desert, miles from anywhere. I hoped Yzz-Five hadn't miscalculated our destination.

Sadie said: 'I'm cold. And the air smells funny.'

I took off my jacket and wrapped it round her.

She was shivering. It was cold. I realized, and she'd feel it more than me because she was used to a hot climate. I sniffed the air. It was breathable — nothing drastic happened to my lungs — but it did have an odd flavour. I tried to place it, and failed. It was an alien scent; the nearest I could get was the reptile house at the zoo, but even that failed to convey the peculiar individuality of it.

I said: 'We might as well look around. Yzz-Five promised the answers to a lot of questions that have been bothering me, but I don't see any guide, nor a signpost. Let's walk that way.'

I waved my hand airily towards nothing in particular. Walking was a slow, tedious business, and quickly became tiring. The sand shifted under our feet and, at times, we sank in it up to our ankles. Sadie stopped, complaining:

'I can't go any further. What's the use, anyway?'

I saw her point. In the twilight, I

couldn't see anything of note. There might be a city or an ocean round he corner; but it was more likely that the desert just went on and on. We seemed to be standing on the top of a slight incline. The ground sloped gently away, devoid of vegetation. I wished it were lighter so that I could see a little more.

'One thing,' I said, 'is certain. We're not on Earth, or Mars. And don't ask me where we are, or how we got here.'

Small whispers of sound drifted on the air. It was an odd noise, like nothing I'd heard before. Very low in pitch, so low I found myself straining to hear it — a cross between a hissing and a slithering. It was an unpleasant sound.

Sadie cuddled closer.

'Alec — I'm frightened!'

I held her tight. She was everything warm and soft in a world I did not understand and I wanted to hold on to her forever. I tried to comfort her.

'There's nothing to worry about,' I said, trying hard to believe my own words. 'Yzz-Five said we needn't feel afraid. I'm with you, darling, and I love you very much. I won't let anything harm you.'

She was quivering. I was probably shaking myself, but I didn't think about that. This seemed an unfriendly world and Yzz-Five wasn't here to reassure us. I found myself doubting if he had ever existed. The sounds grew louder, moving closer. The reptilian smell increased in pungency. In the twilight, something moved, heaving its ungainly bulk towards us.

I couldn't see clearly and, for the first time, I was glad of the poor light. Somehow, I didn't want to see whatever it was coming for us — I had the feeling my sanity would snap if I got one good look at inhabitants of this world.

What I did see was enough to raise the short hairs on the back of my neck. There was a suggestion of animal form, something crossbred between a nightmare and the delusion of a lunatic mind. It was *not human*, not of Earth. Horror pricked my brain and set me trembling. Sadie began to moan.

The stench of alien bodies caught at

my stomach. I felt physically sick, wanted to retch. The hissing, slithering sound became louder, more insistent.

'Something touched me!' Sadie cried out.

Then she fainted clean away. I didn't have the strength to support her and she slid through my arms to the ground. I bent over her, shaking her, calling her to get up. She did not move. I turned, half-crouching to face the alien horror. I swore in a low, ceaseless voice that went on and on . . .

I had the sensation of something reaching out for my mind — an obscene thing crept into my brain and crawled around there. It was an intensification of the feeling I had received from Lingstrom; a contact of minds, revolting, sickening. I felt my consciousness slipping under unbearable mental pressure. Physical contact followed. Something dry and rasping and palpitating fumbled over me, inducing such terror in me as I had never before experienced. Then I blacked out.

How much time elapsed before I regained consciousness I have no idea.

Even then, it seemed I did not wake completely, but hovered on the edge of sleep. I was aware of a swaying motion, of the feel of unclean matter in contact with my flesh. The alien smell was overpowering. I opened my eyes to the twilight gloom — and closed them quickly. I was being carried across the desert and I did not want to see the thing that carried me.

I called: 'Sadie . . . Sadie?' and thought I heard her answer, but could not be sure.

My memories of that nightmare journey are indistinct. I lay in a semi-stupor, frightened, beyond reasoning. Terror welled up inside me. I think that I cried at times, for my face itched and my mouth tasted of salt. I dropped into the pit of darkness, woke again to the swaying rhythm, the alien smell, and fell into darkness yet again.

The motion stopped. I was at rest, lying on hard, cold ground. There was no light at all, not even the gloom that had existed over the desert. I reached out my hand and touched a wall. I was in a building of some sort . . . and Sadie?

I called her name. She was there, lying

beside me, half-conscious. I crawled towards her, touched her; she was shivering. We clung together, comforting each other.

'Alec!' she whispered. 'We're not alone — there's something in here, with us!'

My flesh crawled. Again came that mental finger probing at my brain. The alien smell intensified. Sadie was right — we were not alone. I held her tight, shaking with fear, glad of the darkness that prevented me from seeing the form of the alien thing,

I thought nothing worse could happen to me now. I was wrong. Our ordeal had scarcely begun. If I had known what was to come, I think I should have gone mad.

The telepathic inquisition started. My body was paralysed and I remained incapable of the slightest movement until the end. And I could not resist the intruding mind of the alien by concentrating on thoughts of Sadie, as I had with Lingstrom. I was up against a stronger will. It destroyed my resistance with a single, overwhelming thought . . . then the torture started.

It felt as if *I* had been forced into one insignificant corner of my brain, imprisoned while the alien took possession of my most intimate thoughts. My memory was ravished of all knowledge. Something else lived in my skull now, something shocking. The alien probed every corner of my mind, reading thoughts as I would a book — turning them over, sifting, sorting, tabulating, absorbing. I was helpless against a will of incredible strength.

But the telepathy was not entirely a one-way experience; some of the alien's thoughts leaked through to my isolated corner.

. . . Earth's defences . . . attack from Mars . . . war . . . extend power . . . invade and subjugate . . . expand the empire . . . dominate all worlds . . . all planets . . . Earth's defences . . . search the Earthman's brain . . .

Horrified, I realized at last to what use I was being put, and tried to fight back, to stop this stealing of vital information from my mind. It seemed the alien had temporarily relaxed its iron control. I

119

could feel myself slipping back into that larger portion of my brain — then I screamed, not out loud, but inside my head. A soundless, terrifying scream that echoed through every cell of my body. The alien was still there.

He blasted me with a single thought, sent me whimpering back to my corner, beaten. I knew, then, that with one wave of thought he could destroy me utterly. I was more helpless than a new-born baby in the path of a tank.

The probing went on, digging into my thoughts, searching out the relevant detail. And, as a secret agent, I knew things about Earth's defences that were not made public. I really knew things that would help an alien invasion. I cursed myself bitterly; if only I could forget . . . but that was impossible. The data was there, inscribed on the cells of my brain; there, for the alien to read with his telepathic powers. And I could do nothing.

That insidious mental probing continued, sifting relentlessly my stock of memories, taking what was needed and rejecting the rest. I lived an eternity of unbelievable horror, devoid of all physical sensation, unable to control even the least of my normal muscular activities. Literally, I was unable to lift my little finger.

Like an automaton checking the circuits of some complex machine, the alien examined my brain cell by cell — while I cowered in the small fragment left to me, like a small boy forced to stand in the corner of a classroom for punishment. The inquisition ended abruptly, with the alien's withdrawal from my mind.

I became overburdened with the new feel of my body. I collapsed, sweating and moaning, my limbs shaking uncontrollably. A tension strained every fibre of me. Slowly, I sank into oblivion . . .

I opened my eyes to darkness with an acute awareness of danger. The alien smell still filled the room. I called to Sadie, but she did not answer. I reached out my hand and touched her; and withdrew quickly. She was cold, stiff — and paralysed. She was undergoing the treatment I had received.

I lay still, afraid to move. Somewhere in the pitch black of our prison, only a few feet away, squatted the monstrous form of the alien. I closed my eyes and prayed — prayed that Sadie would come out of it unharmed. I thought of Yzz-Five, and cursed him. 'Nothing to fear,' he had said. *Nothing to fear . . .*

Fear was a living thing that coiled about me. It reached through the darkness and touched me with icy fingers. It chilled the blood in my veins and froze the sweat that oozed through the pores of my skin to crawl down my face. It left me weak and trembling, incapable of forming a decision.

Silently I cursed Yzz-Five for delivering me to this alien world, cursed him long and bitterly. It seemed I could hope for nothing now. Undoubtedly, as soon as the alien had finished with Sadie, we should both be killed; there could be no reason for keeping us alive. It surprised me that I had not already been destroyed.

It was cold, lying there on the ground in that dark cell. I shivered; and remembered I had given my coat to

Sadie. I reached out and touched her again; she was like a person embalmed. I closed my eyes: I was afraid of seeing the thing that crouched in blackness beside me.

Was Yzz-Five one of them? It seemed incredible — but what other explanation could there be? Or had he miscalculated the destination of our fantastic journey? He had called himself a friend and promised explanations ... instead it appeared that death would claim us on this alien world.

I heard a low, whimpering sound. It was Sadie, crying; I knew then that the alien had finished with her. Was this the end for us? I took Sadie in my arms and comforted her. She clung to me, her tear-wet face buried against my chest. I lifted her head, gently, and kissed her.

'What was it?' she muttered. 'Alec, what was it?'

'Don't think about it,' I said. 'Try to forget what's happened.'

The reptilian smell lessened. I could smell Sadie's perfume as her hair brushed my cheek. In the dark, it seemed strange to think of her having green hair, of being Martian. Nothing mattered, except the fact that she was the woman I loved — and soon we should both die.

'What will they do to us now?' she asked.

I didn't answer. I didn't know the answer, for certain.

She said: 'Will we ever get away from this dreadful place, Alec?'

'I don't know,' I said.

'There must be a way out, there must!'

I hesitated about striking a match. The alien might not have left and, above all else, I didn't want to see the detail of his nonhuman shape. I decided to risk it. I struck a match.

We were alone, in a cell of hard earth, roughly square, with a low roof. There was no sign of a door or other exit. I had a grim thought; we might be left to starve, or die of thirst. I began to attack the walls, but they were rock-hard and I made no impression on them. There was no way out; we could only wait for what was in store for us.

Sadie started to cry again. We huddled

together in the dark. I remembered the alien's thoughts that had come to me while I was under telepathic ordeal. The aliens were planning to conquer Earth, to invade the solar system and dominate the planets. The stepping-off point was Mars.

I began to understand then. It was these aliens who were insidiously fomenting war-fever on Mars, working up the colonists against Earth. This was the opening gambit for a large-scale invasion; the Earth-Mars war was merely a cover for something bigger. And I was a pawn in the game.

The knowledge came too late for me to use. I was uneasy. What new horror was to follow the war between Earth and Mars? What were the aliens planning? It seemed I should never know . . . the sands of time were running out. Death appeared inevitable, and there was no way I could help prevent the war, imprisoned on a strange world.

The change came suddenly, without warning. One moment, I was in darkness, holding on to Sadie; the next. I was in a lighted room. Sadie stood beside me. There was a man in the room. A small man with nondescript features who looked as if he might be related to Yzz-Five.

9

Dimensional worlds

The room appeared to be a duplicate of Yzz-Five's hideaway on Mars, even to the scientific apparatus it contained. And again, there was no apparent way out. The small man said:

'Welcome to Yzzolda — that is the name of our world. I am Yzz-One. You may rest here. Reassure yourselves that you are safe — '

'That's what Yzz-Five told us,' I said grimly. 'And look what happened to us!'

'Yzz-Five made a slight miscalculation,' the small man replied. 'He judged that you would be better able to withstand the ordeal; an error of judgment, no more — but it was necessary that you have direct experience of the enemy. Now you will believe the truth of what I must tell you. Sit down and relax. You are safe now, and there is no need for your recent experience to be repeated. When I have finished I shall return you to Mars, for it is there that the final battle must be fought and won.'

I looked at Sadie. It was nice to see her again. She sat down, and I turned to give my attention to Yzz-One.

'Yzzolda,' he began, 'is not in the universe of which your own Earth and Mars are part. It is not in 'space', as you think of it. You must try not to think of space as being limited to three dimensions — the physical dimensions of length, breadth and height. That is not to say this view is wrong, merely that it is not the whole truth.'

Yzz-One paused, looking from me to Sadie; his expression indicated doubt of our ability to understand him. I sympathized with his doubts.

'The concept of hyperspace can only be expressed, finally, by mathematics. For that reason, I can only give you analogies, which cannot convey the finer points of the theory; words are not suitable tools for expressing the precise meaning of mathematics. Hyperspace, as we of

Yzzolda know it, is built up of *infinite* dimensions — and includes your three dimensions of 'space'. Again there is a difficulty with words; the idea of infinite dimensions, each containing a universe similar to that which your telescopes show, does not mean an extension of *space* in the absolute sense. That would be impossible.'

'These dimensions of hyperspace co-exist with each other, interlocking. so that Yzzolda and a myriad other worlds exist in the emptiness described by your limited view of 'space'. They remain, of course invisible — and can only be detected by a mechanics based on hyperspatial mathematics. Try to think of Yzzolda as existing in the interstices between the atomic structure of your 'matter'. Or, if you prefer the image, as existing in the same space at a different level of energy vibration.'

I held on to my head.

'You mean,' I suggested tentatively, 'that Yzzolda and Mars are two worlds inhabiting the same space — that is, the same hyperspace?'

Yzz-One frowned.

'That is not quite what I mean. In your three-dimensional sense of reality, they exist in the same 'space'; the apparent contradiction is due to your limited application of a particular view of the universe. In hyperspatial terms. Yzzolda and Mars are but two of many worlds co-existing at different energy levels.'

Sadie interrupted impatiently: 'This would be very interesting if it was relevant; but what has it to do with us having our minds invaded by that — that thing, whatever it was?'

Yzz-One said: 'A great deal, as you will learn. May I take it you accept my view of hyperspace?'

I nodded. 'Sure. I'm not saying I understand it, but I'll accept your word for it if the idea gets us anywhere.'

Yzz-One continued: 'Very well. You will accept, then, that Mars in your universe is the point of contact with Yzzolda in ours. Yzz-Five, who is working directly under my orders, selected you two for instruction; it was for that reason he transmitted you to Yzzolda. When you entered the cabinet of the vibratory

130

transmitter, you crossed hyperspace, passing through many dimensions to reach Yzzolda. That is the simple explanation of the strange sights you saw.'

I remembered the kaleidoscope of changing worlds, and said: 'But there was no air. How could we live?'

'In hyperspace, there is no time. You lived, because, by your standards, the transition was instantaneous. The fact that it did not seem so was an illusion. You are creatures used to considering time, therefore it was natural you should imagine the journey to last in time.'

I said: 'Let's get one thing straight. I'm only interested in preventing a war between Earth and Mars. Anything else is of purely theoretical interest.'

Yzz-One smiled. 'Your interest is known and approved of. We, too, are intending to stop the war — but for a different and more important reason. A reason you will agree with. Briefly stated, it is to stop an invasion of your whole system.'

I remembered the alien's thoughts that

had come to me. It felt like someone walking over my grave.

'There are still things which need explaining,' I said. 'Where do you and Yzz-Five come into it?'

'To explain that, you must allow me to tell you something of Yzzolda's history. We are a long-lived race, with quite different talents to your own. At no time have we shown much interest in the purely material sciences; your spaceships and atomic physics and engineering and chemical sciences are new to us. New, and a little overwhelming. We do not despise them; it is simply that they are unnatural to us.'

Yzz-One paused, regarding Sadie and me quizzically.

He said: 'You have both experienced examples of our science, the science of the mind. We use telepathy and teleportation and derivatives of these as you use radio and mechanically-propelled vehicles; the power of thought is as natural to us as the power of the atom is to you. It is in this sphere that we have developed far more than any other race with whom we have come into contact. It is a power that gives us tremendous advantages — and certain disadvantages, as you will hear.

'You must know that there are two rival factions on Yzzolda. One group, led by the Emperor; a rebel group, led by myself. It was, incidentally, the Emperor in person who invaded the privacy of your minds a little while back. Of course, the Emperor's group is the more powerful; my own is very much in the minority but, from your point of view, of considerable importance. I will explain that.'

Yzz-One pursed his lips, searching for the right words, the phrases that would have meaning for us.

'I have told you that our development has largely concentrated on our mental powers, to the exclusion of the more material aspects of life. This has had the unfortunate result of deluding certain members of the race into believing that mental superiority is all that matters. They believe that because we are mental giants, then that indicates we are the fittest to survive — not only to survive, but to govern. They forget that other races have developed as far in their own way as we have in ours. To the Emperor's followers, intellect is everything.

'You can, perhaps, guess what has happened. In every contact with other races, the Emperor and his followers have used the power of thought to impress their way of life on others not their mental equals. It has not been a contact for mutual advantage, but one of conquest and subjugation. And this has been going on for many generations.'

I had a sinking feeling in the pit of my stomach. Having had experience of the Emperor's mental abilities, I began to realize we were up against something superhuman. The thought of these aliens over-running Earth was unpleasant in the extreme.

Yzz-One continued: 'At this time, the power of the Emperor extends throughout our universe. It is the greatest empire that has ever been, a galactic empire in the true sense of the term. All races on all worlds are under the Emperor's law. A single thought of his can bring annihilation to millions; he is omnipotent. And now, with the galaxy at his feet, he is restless — greedy for greater power. His desire is to expand the empire throughout the worlds of your dimension.

'Already agents of the Emperor are installed on the planet Mars, stirring up a war against Earth. This is deliberate, and for two reasons. First, to take attention from the invasion. Second, to weaken the defences of both Mars and Earth. Once Mars has been subjugated, the Emperor plans to invade Earth. After that, he will spread from one planet to another until, in time, his domain will include all the worlds of your universe.'

It took my breath away. My legs felt weak. The Emperor's plan was the most stupendous design for conquest I had ever come across. It was majestic and terrifying in scope, almost impossible to credit. He made would-be dictators from Earth's history appear like small boys playing a game.

Sadie said: 'It's fantastic!'

'It would seem so to you,' Yzz-One

replied gravely, 'but remember, the Emperor's power already extends through one galaxy. And nothing can stand before the power of pure thought.'

I was thinking of the time element. Yzz-One had said the race was long-lived; even so, that one being could consider conquering all the planets circling stars throughout the universe was a little beyond my mental grasp. Clearly, the aliens were not even remotely human.

Yzz-One spoke again.

'You must not think of the Emperor's forces as destructive. He does not destroy in the sense that you understand. He subjugates all races to his own ends. No one can stand against him. Where there is active resistance, he kills, as a surgeon cuts away diseased material; but his intention is to rule all others. His ego is such that he cannot bear the idea of any race of beings existing except under his orders.

'Thought, you must understand, is instantaneous; that is how we can get from one planet to another so quickly. We have the ability of teleporting our material bodies through space. And his thought-control, once enforced, is grafted onto lesser minds forever. There is no escape once the Emperor has claimed any being for his own.'

'And you,' I said. 'Where do you come into this? What is your group after?'

It had crossed my mind that we might be exchanging one devil for another.

Yzz-One answered: 'There are a few of us who believe that each race should develop its own talents in its own way. That is why we rebelled, why we are prepared to aid you in the fight against the Emperor. It is too late for that in our own dimension, but not in yours. It appears to us that the Emperor's designs are against the natural scheme of existence. Throughout many worlds, we have seen great diversity of thought and purpose; now all that is ended. Only the Emperor's will exists.

'Many times we have seen races die out because they could no longer evolve in a way natural to them. That the Emperor should deny this right to others, force them into a copy of our own mould, seems to us a crime against the very act of creation. And we are determined that this shall not happen again, to the different races of your dimension.

'You were brought here to learn from your own experience, deliberately handed to the Emperor so that you would believe. If this seems cruel, ask yourselves: would you have believed if you had not this experience?'

I asked myself, and had to admit that Yzz-One was right. Even now I found myself doubting.

Sadie said: 'But how can we fight back against such a being? You say the races of your galaxy have succumbed — what chance have we?'

'Without my help — none. You see, part of the Emperor's success is due to the element of surprise. Others doubt, and, while doubting, are lost. But you believe — and when you return to your own dimension, you will spread the truth. I mentioned that our peculiar develop-ment has disadvantages; this is even more apparent when compared with your highly materialistic evolution. The Emperor's forces, though powerful mentally, still have material bodies — and those bodies can be destroyed by atom bombs and other such weapons which you possess in abundance.

'But suppose no one believed the truth; then those weapons would never be used. That is the kernel of the problem. Once the danger has been realized, the invasion recognized for what it is, then the Emperor is doomed. He must retreat to his own dimension. To you, it will seem ludicrous that one who is so much further advanced than yourselves in mind can be beaten so easily. But it is a fact. We have nothing to withstand the forces of the atom which you can let loose. That is the inevitable penalty for a one-sided development over many generations.'

I cheered up a bit. For the first time, I saw a ray of hope. Earth might yet give a full account of itself and avoid becoming a slave race to the aliens. Yzz-One damped my feelings with his next words.

'Do not imagine that all you have to do is return to Mars and tell what has happened to you. How will you convince others? Your story is fantastic — and agents of the Emperor are already there, sowing the seeds of war. You will be in considerable personal danger. Once those agents find you, you will be ruthlessly killed. No; you still need my help in this matter, and that will be readily given. I hope that, together, we may save your peoples from complete annihilation.'

There was silence in the room. I looked at Sadie; her eyes were half-closed and she was deep in thought. I looked round the room, marvelling at the strange machines that presumably were controlled by pure thought. And I looked at Yzz-One, carefully.

He was such an ordinary looking man; small, quiet, unassuming, with features that would be hard to pick out in a crowd. Yet his words took my breath away and left me gasping. I wondered about him, and Yzz-Five — and the Emperor. Somehow. I got the idea there was more to him than my senses recorded; it was an odd sensation, and put me on edge.

I said: 'I suppose you must be a member of one of the races which the

Emperor and his followers have con-
quered? Yet you talk as if — well — as if
you were.'

I didn't quite know how to finish the
sentence. What I had in mind seemed
impossible, looking at him, so ordinary in
a grey suit. Sadie opened her eyes wide. I
saw the colour of them; copper — and a
light of alarm.

'Yes,' she breathed, 'that is what has
been bothering me. Just what are you,
Yzz-One?'

The small man hesitated slightly.

'You must prepare for a shock,' he said.
He paused, then; 'I am of the same race
as the Emperor. My physical form is
precisely the same.'

Sadie gave a little gasp and came
upright from her chair. I looked at her
because, suddenly, I didn't want to look
at Yzz-One any more. Her face was white.

I said, mechanically: 'That's impossible.'

I was thinking back to the moment in
the desert, soon after our arrival on
Yzzolda, when I had glimpsed an alien
through the twilight, I remember its

nonhuman aspect, the feel of it as I had been carried over the desert. I couldn't believe that Yzz-One was like that . . . then I realized that I did not want to believe. It was a thought that made me shudder.

The small man said, calmly: 'It is true. I have precisely the same form as the Emperor.'

Sadie said: 'But the smell?'

'What you see now, a man of your own race, is purely an illusion. My form would horrify you, so I adopt this guise to shield you. It is a simple matter of impressing a mental image on your brains — you think you see me, that's all. As for smell . . . let me, for a moment, relax my control over that part of your brains which deals with olfactory sensations.'

I held my breath automatically, but I couldn't keep it up. When I did breathe air into my lungs I almost choked. A reptilian smell, pungent, sickening, filled the room. Then, in a moment, it was gone.

Yzz-One smiled.

'You see? You do not doubt now?'

Sadie had crept right up to me. She slipped her hand into mine. I held it tight.

'I hope,' I said shakily, 'that you never let the control slip completely, so that we see you as you are.'

'Have no fear,' Yzz-One assured us. 'To me, this telepathic illusion is easily sustained . . . besides I should have no use for you — insane!'

10

Return to Mars

Tension filled the room. My nerves were high-strung, my muscles taut, quivering. I had a moment of claustrophobia, and wanted to scream and beat the walls with my bare hands. I felt hemmed in, a prisoner in that underground cell with no door. I wanted to leave the strange world of Yzzolda forever, to return to my own dimension and forget all I had learned.

Yzz-One leaned against a cabinet surrounded by helices and cables; behind him, I saw a duplicate of the machine with star-shaped wafers of metal. He leaned there, smiling at us, small and ordinary and dressed in a grey suit. His smile was an illusion. He was an illusion. He was alien.

I felt Sadie's fingernails dig into the palm of my hand. I put my arm about her and felt better. Yzz-One watched us closely. He said: 'Do not fear me. I am your friend. The fact that I was given a shape that horrifies you signifies nothing. Do not think about that. Remember we are fighting a common enemy — the Emperor.'

He was right. I pulled myself together. My job was to prevent a war between Earth and Mars; now, that took on another aspect — to stop an invasion of the whole galaxy by alien beings.

'All right. What do we do now?' I said.

'There are still things you need to know,' Yzz-One stated. 'The Emperor's followers are already established on Mars. They are disguised as men and therefore difficult for you to recognize. Undoubtedly, they will be in key positions; in the government, in the army, in the radio and television stations that broadcast propaganda — and they will be hard to get at. Yzz-Five will help you there.'

I remembered the telepathic probing of Lingstrom. Yzz-One was right again. If the aliens could carry off such a deception they were really dangerous.

I said: 'Lingstrom is one of them.'

I thought back to my interview with Oving. He, too, perhaps . . .

Sadie interrupted. 'Lingstrom can't be. He's the head of Martian Intelligence. He's well-known. I mean, how could — '

Yzz-One said: 'Such a deception would be easy to one of our race. First, the man to be used would be killed, his body destroyed. The Emperor's agent would then replace him, using telepathic control to impress the original image of the man on those around him. I assure you it is not at all difficult.'

Sadie said: 'I still can't believe it — not Lingstrom.'

'He's a telepath all right,' I told her. 'He got inside my mind without any trouble.' Another thought occurred to me; I turned to Yzz-One. 'You and Yzz-Five — did you kill to create your illusions?'

'No. That was not necessary as we were not intending to replace living men. Our illusions are simply to hide us from the people of Mars — and from agents of the Emperor. What we did was to build up a composite image from men we observed in the street, taking an average of

146

individual features for our purpose.'

I nodded; that accounted for the ordinariness of Yzz-Five and Yzz-One. It was a point that had worried me — and the solution was simple.

Sadie asked: 'How could Yzz-Five convey me from my bungalow to his hideaway? It seemed there was no delay; just a sudden change.'

'A development of teleportation. Normally, we can teleport ourselves at a thought — no machine is necessary. But with non-telepaths, such as yourselves, it is necessary to use a machine to amplify the thought-command. The power needed to move matter is considerable when that matter does not help the action in any way.'

So Yzz-Five had just *thought* himself out of the runabout the first time I had seen him. And again, he had teleported himself through the wall when I had encountered him at the meeting. But he could not teleport us without a mechanical aid.

I said: 'These cells without doors. I suppose you used a machine to bring us

147

through the walls?'

'That is correct.' Yzz-One smiled faintly. 'I keep forgetting that teleportation seems strange to you. To us, the power of mind over matter is an everyday affair, something we take for granted.'

'I suppose,' I said, 'it is a development of your trick of crossing dimensions?'

'Not quite the same. We cannot cross from Yzzolda to Mars without a machine to amplify the power of thought. To transmit our material bodies from one point in space to another is easy; a simple change of energy level is required. Or if you prefer it, the atoms of our bodies pass through the space between atoms of other matter. Distance makes no difference to the transmission.'

Yzz-One looked at his machines.

'I had to use a mechanical aid to bring you from the cell of the Emperor; that was because you were unable to aid me with your minds. But we have more important things to discuss. Yzz-Five waits on Mars for your return. He, and other agents of mine are ready to combat the Emperor's forces. You must return immediately.'

That was good news to me. I was beginning to be afraid I'd never get back to my own dimension, where you had to open a door to get through a wall. Sadie gave a sigh of relief.

'This hatred the Martians have for Earthmen,' I said. 'It's artificial, of course — but how is it done?'

'Agents of the Emperor broadcast a wave of thought which is picked up by the Martians. This thought wave is one of hatred directed at Earth; probably they use some mechanical aid to amplify it. The hate-thought is impressed on the brains of the Martians until they come to believe it natural to them; and each broadcast increases its potency, bringing the danger of war nearer.'

I thought that over. Yes, that and the orators at mass-meetings, and the drums — together they would make a powerful weapon to warp the will of the Martian people. I looked at Sadie and grinned suddenly.

'Darling,' I said, 'isn't it obvious? You never really hated me at all. It was just a thought impressed on you by the aliens!'

She clung to me, her eyes shining.

'Alec — of course!'

Yzz-One regarded us, baffled.

'She never hated you,' he agreed. 'It is easy to read her thoughts. She loves you. It was because of this affinity between you, a man of Earth and a woman of Mars, that you were selected to learn the truth. Now, your planets will fight together against the Emperor.' He stopped short, then added: 'Though this affinity is one I shall never understand.'

I kissed Sadie just to show him how it worked; then I realized what he had said. It was another shock.

'You mean,' I said, incredulously, 'that you don't understand love?'

Yzz-One shook his head sadly.

'I can read your thoughts, but they mean nothing. It is outside my experience. Your relationship is beyond me — or any of our race.'

I remembered how Lingstrom had been revolted by my thoughts of Sadie. It still seemed incredible. I stared at Yzz-One, feeling sorry for him. He might be a mental giant, but . . . well, I could do without telepathy while I had Sadie.

I said: 'Surely, on a biological basis, alone — '

'You do not understand. We of Yzzolda are one sex; or, if you prefer it, we have no sex. That is why I cannot comprehend your feelings. They do not make sense.'

'No sex,' I echoed. 'But you must reproduce yourselves somehow. All animals — '

'We have no sex,' Yzz-One replied. 'No sympathetic relationship such as you know. Each of us is capable of reproducing our kind, and this we do by a thought process involving the voluntary splitting of body cells. Where there was one, there are two. That is all. And the new being is not newborn in your sense. There is no parent and no child; simply two beings, identical, where there was only one before. Of course, the sameness disappears as both beings undergo different experiences in different environments.'

Sadie's face wrinkled in an expression of distaste.

'It sounds disgusting,' she said coldly.

I thought about it. Other worlds would have other customs; it was not so strange really. But, looking at Sadie, I was glad I came from our own world.

I said: 'But surely, there must be some feeling between two members of your race, immediately after cell-fission?'

'None. On Yzzolda, each being is a separate, self-satisfying entity. We have no feelings corresponding to yours. Your love for each other is incomprehensible to me, utterly outside my experience; but it is useful — because it exists, I am able to resolve the differences between two worlds. You will stand together to face the Emperor's threat.'

Yzz-One paused, looking at us.

'Perhaps it is this love which makes you worthy of continued existence. Because of this, it may be that your race can go its own way. It may be your emotional life that sets you apart from all other races; it may be . . . I do not know. Certainly this experience is new to us of Yzzolda and it would be a pity if the Emperor's forces were to destroy such a precious and fragile thing.'

I felt like laughing. That Yzz-One should think of human love as 'precious and fragile' struck me as funny. Obviously he had no conception of the strength of the force that linked a man and a woman. For the first time, I felt superior to the beings of Yzzolda. I said: 'Ever since our race began, the power of love has been the greatest influence in a man's life. Reason is as nothing before it. Emotion rules our lives and creates our destiny. That is our strength.'

Sadie gave me an odd look out of the corner of her eyes.

'Are you talking about me, Alec?' she murmured.

I didn't answer that.

'It is a pity you are not able to transmit your thoughts directly to each other,' Yzz-One said. 'It might be interesting if I were to speak aloud the thoughts you each have about the other.'

Sadie blushed, a pinkness colouring her cheeks.

'Don't you dare!' she snapped furiously.

I grinned. 'Perhaps it would be best if

you didn't,' I told Yzz-One. 'We have our own ways of communicating such thoughts. Though I agree — it would be interesting to know just how Sadie feels about me.'

'That,' Sadie Lubinski said, with a toss of her head, 'I'll tell you when we're alone!'

Yzz-One started to make adjustments to the vibratory transmitter, preparatory to sending us back to Mars. He was completely absorbed in his work and it seemed a good moment to straighten things out between Sadie and myself.

'Sadie,' I said, 'I love you. I always have and always will. It's true I'm a secret agent for Earth and that you're a Martian. That makes no difference to the way I feel about you. You accused Earth of preparing to make war against Mars; that's not true. I was sent to Mars to prevent war breaking out. Do you believe me?'

She clung to me, her green hair against my chest, her face upturned. Her copper eyes were moist. She was very lovely, and very dear to me.

'Yes, Alec. I believe you. I didn't at first. I really believed you were one of those intending to crush my people — but I know now that was just a thought impressed on me by the aliens. Can you forgive me doubting your love? Alec, I do love you . . . '

I kissed her hard and felt her tremble in my arms.

She said: 'I suppose you guessed I'm an agent sent to watch you? It doesn't make any difference, does it?'

'No difference, my darling. We're on the same side now, against the Emperor.' An idea occurred to me. 'You were waiting for me at the space port. The agents of the Emperor must have used their telepathic powers to find out about me — yes, that accounts for it.'

'You are right, Mr. Black,' Yzz-One said, looking up from a maze of wiring. 'The Emperor would have no difficulty in learning of your mission,' I hardly heard his words; my mind was on Sadie.

It was as old as Earth itself — and as new as the moment. We both knew the exhilaration of being in love. Nothing else mattered. Sadie cried with happiness, and I told her all over again how much she meant to me. We forgot about Yzz-One and the world of darkness far across the dimensions from Earth and Mars. We forgot about the Emperor and the invasion, till . . .

'The machine is ready,' Yzz-One said suddenly. 'I will return you to Mars.'

I stood up, brought back to the realization that I still had a job to do. I wondered what had happened on Mars since I had been away. I knew a sense of urgency, of time wasting; but there was one more thing I had to say to Sadie before we put our personal feelings to one side.

I caught her hands and turned her towards me. Looking into her eyes, I said, quietly:

'Sadie — when this business is over, if we both come through it, will you be my wife?'

I knew the answer before she spoke. It was in her eyes, shining like a warm light.

She answered: 'Yes. Alec, I will.'

I turned to Yzz-One. 'We're ready now.'

He nodded in understanding. 'Very well. Step into the cabinet.'

The helices were vibrating, glowing. A deep hum came from somewhere in the maze of wiring. We did not say farewell.

I held Sadie's hand tight as we stepped into the cabinet. There was blackness — a blackness that changed, slowly, to a soft, diffused light. There was a void, silent, overwhelming. We were in the borderland between dimensions.

Time had no meaning here. There was only the touch of Sadie's hand on mine in an emptiness of sensation. I knew a moment of terror. Suppose something went wrong? Suppose we never arrived on Mars, but were doomed to wander this infinity of nothingness forever? It was a thought that chilled my blood.

Then I saw the myriad worlds of other dimensions, flickering like images on a screen, tall cities and strange beings, moving like apparitions, always changing. I was struck by the wonder of it. The kaleidoscope of immaterial worlds flashed past and I lost count of all there was to see. I could not believe that all this could exist — or coexist with Mars and Yzzolda. It was too much for the limited imagination of man to grasp.

An incongruous thought came to me; I had left Cosmo Scott facing death in the second chapter of my new book. Suddenly, *Vendetta on Mars* seemed completely irrelevant to my situation. The antics of my fictional hero palled to insignificance before the revelation of Yzzolda and the dimensional worlds of hyperspace. Whether I liked it or not, I had a new conception of reality, and there could be no turning back. Cosmo Scott would never be the same to me again.

Kaleidoscopic images came and went in a blur of constant change. I began to wonder what I would find on Mars. Was I too late to prevent the war? Hurry, hurry, throbbed a voice inside my head, the forces of the Emperor must be stopped. I felt the grip of Sadie's hand in mine and spoke aloud — forgetting there was no air to carry the sound. My mouth made movements but the silence remained. Then we were in a lighted room. Mars — and Yzz-Five.

11

Preliminary skirmish

I could not quite regard Yzz-Five in the same way that I had before the trip to Yzzolda. He looked exactly the same, small, pale-faced, ordinary. Only, now, I knew that he wasn't ordinary — or even a man. He was alien. And I was filled with awe as I stood before him.

Sadie said, casually: 'Well. It's nice to be back.'

She took off my coat and handed it to me; she no longer needed it now that we'd left the cold darkness of that world across the dimensions.

I sat down and looked about the room. It was the same as before. A stone cell underground, with no window and no door. And there was one new machine, as odd-looking as the others. It didn't have any purpose that I could see. An unpleasant idea crept into my mind; if anything happened to Yzz-Five, we were doomed. The lift shaft in the garage had been an illusion. Only he could teleport us to the outside world.

To get rid of the feeling that it gave me, I looked at Sadie. She was sitting back in another chair, more completely relaxed than I could manage after all we'd been through. It was nice to think that she'd be my wife in a short while.

I smiled at her. She smiled back. She turned to Yzz-Five, her expression suddenly grave, and asked: 'Well, what do we do now?'

Her words brought my wandering thoughts back with a jerk. After our experiences on Yzzolda, just to sit there seemed an anticlimax. We ought to be taking action. She had stated the problem at the back of my mind: What *did* we do now?

Yzz-Five said: 'The position has changed since you left Mars. War fever has reached a new peak of intensity. Under the influence of the Emperor's hate-thought, the Martians are eager to begin the war against Earth.'

160

Despite the heat in the room, I shivered. Then I remembered my words to Fisher: 'Keep away for twenty-four hours. After that, take whatever action you think necessary.'

I said: 'How much time have I been away?'

'A little over thirty hours,' Yzz-Five replied. 'But do not worry about your friend, Fisher. I took the precaution of impersonating you, and told him to delay action until you saw him again.'

Thirty hours! I wondered why I wasn't hungry. I'd had nothing to eat or drink in that time.

It had been night time when I went to Martian Exports. Since then, a day and night had passed. Outside, it would be morning again. I was glad that Yzz-Five had forestalled any action on Fisher's part; even though he was a good agent, he did not have the facts that I had. He might have precipitated serious trouble.

Sadie said: 'I suggest you teleport me to the street, Yzz-Five. I'll go to my chief and tell him what I know. Perhaps it isn't too late to stop the war machine — if I can

161

get to responsible people and convince them of the truth.'

I felt my scalp move. My hair stood up.

'No!' I said hurriedly. 'I won't allow it. Lingstrom is one of the Emperor's agents.'

The small man — I couldn't stop myself thinking of Yzz-Five like that — looked from Sadie to me, and back at Sadie.

'I think the suggestion worth trying. After all, Lingstrom is not Miss Lubinski's immediate superior. She will report to a Martian. Lingstrom's orders must come to her through a chain of subordinates.'

'No,' I repeated firmly. It's too dangerous. 'I won't allow it.'

Sadie turned copper eyes on me in a determined stare. Her chin stuck out.

'You can't stop me, Alec. I'm going, with Yzz-Five's help. There won't be any danger — after all, I am an agent for Mars.'

'Then I'll go and see Ross at the same time,' I said. 'If I can — '

Yzz-Five interrupted: 'That would be most foolish, Mr. Black — you are a marked man, known and wanted. You could not take half-a-dozen steps in the open without being recognized. Your death would avail us nothing. You must stay here and Miss Lubinski will go alone. I will prepare the teleportation machine in readiness.'

I watched him stoop over the machine with the glittering star-shaped wafers of metal. He adjusted controls. The vision screen lit up, and the affair of metal wafers began to revolve, reminding me in appearance of a mobile. The star shapes blurred as the revolutions mounted; my eyes were dazzled and I had to look away. Probably the hypnotic effect the machine had was incidental to its purpose, but it existed all the same.

Yzz-Five sat on a chair before the teleportation machine.

He asked: 'Are you ready, Miss Lubinski?'

She replied: 'Yes.'

I kissed her hastily and said: 'Don't take any chances.'

Yzz-Five was silent, concentrating. I watched Sadie. She stood alone in the centre of the room, slim, beautiful . . . then she wasn't there any more. I looked in the vision screen attached to the machine and saw her walking down a street in Marsport.

Even though I had known what to expect, it was still a shock. I blinked, looked at the spot where she had been a moment before, stared again at the screen. The dimensional science of Yzzolda took a little getting used to. Yzz-Five remained the calm, confident operator of powers beyond my understanding.

The street was busy with Martians shopping. I watched as she continued along the street; her lithe form had a swing to it, graceful, sleek. She turned into the doorway of a building that bore no nameplate and showed her pass to the doorman. I didn't need telling this was the headquarters of Martian Intelligence.

Yzz-Five touched another control; sound came from the box next to the vision screen. I heard the doorman's voice:

'You are to report to Room 17

immediately, Miss Lubinski.'

I saw Sadie hesitate.

Yzz-Five said: 'Room 17 is Lingstrom's private sanctum. Obviously he suspects something.'

I bawled at the screen: 'Sadie! Get away now — come back here!'

Yzz-Five was amused; that is, if an alien can be amused by anything.

'She cannot hear you, Mr. Black. You must let events proceed in their own way.'

Sadie made up her mind.

'Very well,' she said, and walked along a corridor.

'Do not worry,' Yzz-Five told me. 'Miss Lubinski is safe. I can bring her back here if danger threatens.'

'Then do it now. Bring her back at once!'

'Not yet, Mr. Black. We may learn something to our advantage.' He repeated: 'Do not worry — I can protect her.'

I was sweating when I saw her open the door to Room 17 and pass inside. The image on the vision screen followed her.

The doorman must have warned Lingstrom that she was coming. He was ready, waiting for her. Oving stood behind the door, a gun in his hand. I held my breath. Surely they wouldn't shoot her down without a chance.

'We are glad to see you, Miss Lubinski,' Oving said. 'More glad than you know. We thought you had slipped through our fingers.'

Sadie's face was a shade paler, but she did not flinch.

'I don't understand,' she answered. 'What do you mean?'

Lingstrom pointed to a chair.

'Sit down,' he said, coldly.

Lingstrom stood over her, tall and thin, stroking his pointed beard. His eyes stared at her in a way that sent ripples of fear racing up and down my spine.

My eyes jerked to another part of the screen. It showed Oving, paunchy and bald, with a hooked nose and hanging lower lip. His reptilian eyes were fixed on Sadie over the gleaming barrel of the gun he pointed at her. You, too, I thought — you're another of *them*.

Lingstrom spoke. 'Where is Mr. Black?'

Sadie shrugged.

'I don't know. I haven't seen him for — '

Lingstrom interrupted her, his voice flat, controlled and emotionless:

'Do not lie to me. I know about your trip to Yzzolda. I am aware that you know the truth about us. Tell me — where is Black hiding? And who has been helping you?'

Sadie didn't answer. Lingstrom drew a gun and held it to her head.

He said: 'You are going to die, Miss Lubinski. But first, answer my questions. If you pretend to know nothing, your death will not be pleasant. Oving, prepare the serum.'

I turned to Yzz-Five. 'Bring her back, damn you! Bring her back, do you hear?'

The small man waved me away.

'In due course, Mr. Black. Please do not interfere — this requires my utmost concentration.'

I had a lump in my throat. Sadie . . .

'You've got to save her,' I pleaded. 'You've got to.'

I watched Oving prepare the hypodermic, filling the cylinder with a red liquid.

167

Lingstrom said: 'I am going to drug you, Miss Lubinski — then I shall be able to probe your mind without interference. When I have the facts I need, you will die. You will not come out of the drug coma. Or you can be sensible and tell me now. That way, your death will be easier. Make up your mind.'

I never knew before that it was possible to be so scared for somebody else. But then no one had ever meant what Sadie did to me now. I was afraid for her. The fear in me was mounting, holding me in the grip of paralysis. My voice came out a hoarse croak.

'Get her out of there!'

Yzz-Five remained calm, almost detached. He said: 'These two agents of the Emperor are not strong. Lingstrom's telepathy needs the aid of a drug to beat down Miss Lubinski's resistance. That is an important point.' He added, for my benefit: 'She is safe. I have constructed a protective shell of thought around her. Soon, I will teleport her to this room.'

Even though he seemed so sure of his power, I was still scared for Sadie. The force binding me to the woman I loved was a weakness now. I watched Oving move forward with the hypodermic.

Lingstrom said: 'Miss Lubinski, you will either answer my questions or submit to such mental torture as will drive you mad. Which is it to be?'

Beside me, Yzz-Five commented: 'Very interesting. If the Emperor's agents were sure of themselves, they would have tried to kill her before this. They are bluffing, trying to make her break down and reveal what she knows. They are worried. That is good — an advantage to us. This interview has been worthwhile.'

He remained calm and analytical and I found myself envious of his self-control.

Sadie replied: 'I'll tell you nothing. I'm a Martian and will not betray my — '

Lingstrom motioned Oving with his hand.

'Use the serum!'

Light flashed on the hypodermic needle as Oving advanced; the serum in the transparent cylinder had an awful fascination for me. I had to force my gaze away from the screen, back to Yzz-Five. The small man was motionless, his face a mask of concentration. I dare not interrupt him now. I prayed he had not left it too late to save Sadie. The star-shaped pieces of metal revolved faster, glittered metallically, blurring with their speed and appearing as a sphere of changing light. Hypnotized, I stared at the teleportation machine. I felt my eyes glaze over, my brain dull. Then —

Sadie's voice broke the spell: 'Hello, Alec.'

I spun round. She stood beside me, unharmed, smiling weakly. Her lips were bright red in contrast to the whiteness of her cheeks, and she was trembling. I caught her in my arms.

'Sadie — darling,' I whispered. 'You're safe!'

Yzz-Five said, calmly: 'She was in no danger.'

I released Sadie and turned to face him.

'No danger!' I said, angrily. 'You cold-blooded monster — I was sweating with fear — and you say she was in no danger!'

Yzz-Five switched off his machine.

'Our standards of conduct are different,' he said. 'That is inevitable because we come from different worlds. It is not to be expected that you will appreciate my point of view — besides, you are emotionally attached to Miss Lubinski. It was natural for you to be afraid for her.'

Sadie said: 'Anyway, thanks for getting me out of there, Yzz-Five. I expected you to bring me back, of course, but I was getting worried about the time you were taking.'

'Your experience has not been futile,' Yzz-Five assured her. 'I have learnt important facts from the behaviour of Lingstrom and Oving. I am grateful to you.'

'Grateful!' I said. 'Why you — '

Sadie snapped: 'Don't keep on about it. Alec. I'm safe now, and that's all that matters. Just try and relax.'

'We must work quickly now,' Yzz-Five began. 'The Emperor's agents know that you are receiving help from my group — but they do not know the details. They do not know how many of us are on

Mars, nor what our plans are. We must strike before they can organize a counter-blow. You will be wondering why Oving did not kill you at that first meeting, Mr. Black. He had the opportunity and knew who you were. It would have been very simple. The reason is that they intended to use you in their game. When you had gathered more information of the Martian war programme, you would have been forcibly deported as an undesirable — and when you made your report to Earth, the position would have looked so bad to your government that they, too, would prepare for war. It was one more step in the Emperor's plan to take attention away from his invasion of your dimension.'

I brooded on that and found little satisfaction in it. It seemed to me that I was a very unimportant piece in a game played for high stakes. My ego suffered. If only the aliens had not found a way to bridge the dimensions between Yzzolda and Mars . . .

Sadie said: 'But what do we do now?

How are we to get the truth to the people?'

'Our problem is two-fold,' Yzz-Five stated. 'First, to identify the Emperor's agents — they will be numerous and in positions of power. Second, to reveal them for what they are to the Martians. We must show the people how they have been used for others' gain — and we have not long in which to act.'

Not long in which to save the universe, I thought — and laughed. This was a situation in which Cosmo Scott would have revelled; but Cosmo Scott's creator was without a plan of any kind. I had to rely on Yzz-Five and his companions.

I said, looking at the small man with new respect: 'I suppose you can identify your own kind by telepathy?'

I thought: We're not fighting for Mars alone — nor even Earth. The Emperor intends to spread through all the worlds of this dimension. The whole of the known universe is in deadly danger. All the races on all the planets revolving about all the stars if we lose the fight on Mars, all these races are doomed. It was a sobering thought.

'Yes, Mr. Black,' Yzz-Five answered. 'I can identify the agents of the Emperor by telepathy — but even that will not be so easy as perhaps you think. Each will be protected by a thought-screen. Their thoughts will, of course, be different from those of the Martians — the difference in attitude towards sex will be sufficient test. But consider the time it would take to test even those officials in high positions. And time is against us. We cannot afford to wait, and I have not enough helpers to hasten this process.'

Sadie said: 'If we could force them into the open somehow — '

Yzz-Five nodded.

'That is indeed the problem — to force them to act before they are ready . . . and I think I know the answer!'

12

Plans and action!

I leaned forward, my eyes fixed on the small, pale figure of Yzz-Five. Even then, knowing what I did, it seemed incredible that he was not what he appeared — a very ordinary man dressed in a conventional grey suit. That I saw only an image impressed on my brain by the power of telepathy, that he was as alien in form as the thing I had half-glimpsed on the dark world of Yzzolda, seemed the most fantastic part of the whole affair.

The blank walls of the room reminded me that we were underground; the machines gave the place an air of mystery. And in this strange place, the three of us — myself, a man of Earth, Sadie, a woman of Mars, and Yzz-Five, an alien creature from another dimension — were trying to save a universe from mental subjugation to that weird being known as the Emperor. Not in my wildest imaginings had I plunged Cosmo Scott into such a desperate situation; the accuracy of the old adage, 'truth is stranger than fiction', was borne home to me.

I listened as Yzz-Five told us his plan.

'I shall need the help of both of you,' he said. 'That is why I transmitted you to Yzzolda. What I propose is this: with the aid of Miss Lubinski, I will select a number of important Martian officials. These will probe for alien thoughts, to prove they are indeed the men they appear, and not agents of the Emperor. Those that are genuine Martians, I will teleport here — and you will tell your story. I can aid you by getting inside their minds, thus proving part of your story — but convincing them of the truth will largely depend on you.'

That sounded all right to me; and I felt better, knowing I had some degree of importance in the scheme of things.

I said: 'And get Ross and Fisher here. If I can convince them, they can get word to Earth and prevent the Terran government from panicking and striking the first blow.'

Yzz-Five nodded.

'That is an important point, Mr. Black.'

I looked at Sadie. She was thinking hard, elbows on her knees, chin cupped by her hands. She straightened up, and said:

'We need a representative cross-section of Martian life. From what you and Yzz-One have told us, I feel it would be useless approaching the heads of government departments — they will almost certainly be aliens. We might try one or two Under-Secretaries in Civil Service posts. Then we'll want well-known scientists; they'll understand about this dimension business — '

Yzz-Five interrupted: 'Yes, we must include a mathematician.'

' — and a popular TV broadcaster,' Sadie continued, 'and leaders of the Workers' Trade Union. We'll want women, too. I suggest the President of the Martian Women's Council, and someone from the Feminine Cultural League.'

'Don't forget the armed forces,' warned

Yzz-Five. 'Surely the Emperor's agents have not taken over all the important roles? An odd General or so should help. And there must be a few lesser officials in the government who are still Martian.'

'My helpers will investigate all these people,' Yzz-Five said. 'Those who are on our side will be transmitted here for you to work on.'

'Your helpers,' I said. 'How many are they?'

'Too few for the task — and the agents of the Emperor outnumber us. But we will do our best.'

Sadie looked worried. I asked her what the trouble was.

'It's this,' she said. 'Yzz-Five was able to watch my movements from a distance, and he had no difficulty in locating Oving and Lingstrom. Surely they can find us, here?'

I didn't like that idea. I felt the return of fear, and looked to Yzz-Five for reassurance.

'It is a danger,' he admitted. 'But remember, I knew where to look.

Lingstrom and the others are playing the part of men in official posts, while we are in hiding. They will not find it so easy to locate this underground cell.'

It sounded too good to me. I said:

'Can't they detect your thought-waves?'

'They could — but neither easily nor quickly, Mr. Black. You are thinking in terms of radio waves — thought is subtler than that. Undoubtedly, the agents of the Emperor are even now probing for this hideaway; the chances of their success are not high. Thought-waves are broadcast on a tight beam, not spread out and radiating — with luck, we shall avoid discovery until it is too late for the enemy to move against us.'

I tried to sound casual about my next question.

'And if they are lucky? If they do find us — what then?'

Yzz-Five replied: 'Do not fear, Mr. Black. This hideaway is protected by a screen of thought. They cannot harm us. You are quite safe.'

I wasn't convinced. I'd felt the Emperor's strength once and wasn't keen on experiencing that mental contact again.

I said: 'All right. So we bring some Martians here and convince them of the truth. What happens after that?'

Yzz-Five smiled gently.

'You are forgetting what Yzz-One told you. Our race has no material science nor weapons of war such as your race possesses — and our bodies can still be destroyed by atom bombs. Once your people believe the truth, that Mars is invaded by aliens, then the Emperor will withdraw across the dimensions. He must withdraw — or have his forces blasted out of existence. You may feel sure that the danger is past once the Emperor's agents have been exposed. Now I must concentrate my thoughts; please do not disturb me.'

I watched Yzz-Five seat himself in a relaxed position. He closed his eyes. I thought: this is a helluva way to fight a war! It irritated me that such an ordinary-looking man should take control of my affairs.

I became aware that he had restarted

the teleportation machine. He must be carrying out a thought-probe of Martian officials, I reflected. It was strange to think of the small man and his helpers sending out thought-waves, prying into the brains of Martians, listening in on their most intimate secrets.

Then a familiar voice said: 'Won't you introduce me to your lady friend, Alec?'

Fisher had arrived, his barrel-shaped body topped by a red face and a bristle of moustache. He looked amazed at his sudden arrival in the room.

I turned to Yzz-Five and saw him concentrated on his machine. Fisher stared curiously round the room, his gaze returning to Sadie.

I made the introductions: 'Sadie Lubinski, secret agent for Mars, now engaged to marry me — Ralph Fisher, chief of Terran Intelligence Service on Mars, now under my orders.'

Their eyes met, fencing, distrustful. Fisher said, politely:

'I suppose I should congratulate you, Alec. Will you tell me what this is about — and, particularly, by what brand of magic I arrived here?'

I started to explain, stopped as a new arrival was teleported into the hideaway. It was Ross. The resident ambassador appeared startled. His eyes flicked from Sadie, to Yzz-Five, to the strange machines; he was scared and suspicious.

He said, stiffly: 'Mr. Black, I insist on knowing what this means.'

'You'll get the answers in a short while,' I answered him. 'We're waiting for some other guests before getting down to business.'

Ross stood silent. His smooth manner was ruffled, and he seemed unsure of himself. Just then, a Martian walked through the wall. Ross began to sweat, and I felt sorry for him. Other Martians arrived. The room began to be crowded.

There was a babble of voices, a tension, bewilderment on many faces. The Martians herded together at one end of the room, Fisher and Ross stood close to me, the only other Earthmen in the room; both regarded Sadie suspiciously. I waited for Yzz-Five.

At last, the small man spoke.

'All are here, Mr. Black. All, that is, who are not of the enemy. You may tell your story now.'

I stood up. 'First of all,' I said, to the astonished crowd, 'you must understand one thing. You have been brought here for one purpose only; to save our universe from an invasion of alien beings. In effect, that means — stop the threatened war between Earth and Mars.'

I paused, looking round me. Yes, I had their attention. I introduced myself, and Sadie. I looked at Yzz-Five. How could I make them understand about him? Yzz-Five solved the problem for me. I sensed his thoughts penetrate to my brain, and knew that everyone else in the room was receiving the same message.

I am an alien from another world, the world of Yzzolda, far across the dimensions. What you see is a telepathic image impressed on your brains. The reason for this illusion is that my natural form would appear so horrific to your eyes that your reason would give way. I am not speaking to you in words, but projecting my thoughts directly into your minds.

There was a stunned silence. Neither Earthmen nor Martians were used to receiving communications by telepathy. When Yzz-Five finished, I said:

'You were brought here to this room, from your different offices and workshops and homes, by the power of thought. Yzz-Five uses teleportation as you and I use a runabout.'

Again I paused, judging their reaction. I went on to tell them why the Terran Government had sent me to Mars, and how I had met Sadie. I told them of my adventures, of the meeting with Lingstrom and Oving, and how Yzz-Five had transmitted me to Yzzolda.

Yzz-Five used telepathy again, explaining the theory of hyperspace, the worlds contained within the dimensions. Argument broke out among the scientists, but it was the mathematician who had the last word.

'Such a theory is not new to us,' he said. 'What is new is that the theory should be proven by experience. To me, this revelation of interlocked worlds is most interesting. I have no doubt whatever of the truth of the communication we have just received.'

I told them of my meeting with the Emperor and how my brain had been robbed of all knowledge. I described the horror of it, and my first realization of the Emperor's purpose. I went on to Yzz-One and the rebel group, how they were helping us against the Emperor.

The Martians were muttering amongst themselves; disbelief was plain in their faces. Sadie said:

'It's true. Every word is true — I was there, too. You must listen, and believe. If you don't believe, the aliens will win.'

I took up the story again, to tell them of the Emperor's power, of his galactic empire in the universe across the dimensions. I told of his intention to rule our universe, to subjugate all races to his will. I emphasized his incredible mental ability.

Ross was staring at me as if I were mad; even Fisher showed his doubt of my sanity. I went on again speaking faster. I described how agents of the Emperor had taken over the high positions of government on Mars to prepare for war against

Earth. I told of the alien thought-waves broadcasting a message of hatred to work up the people of Mars against Earth — and I emphasized that this war was nothing but a trick to mask the real invasion and weaken our defences.

Sadie spoke again: 'I went to Yzzolda with Alec and I know that he speaks the truth. You must believe, no matter how strange it sounds. Mars and Earth must work together — with Yzz-Five and his helpers — to stop the Emperor. If we fail, then every race throughout our universe is doomed to mental slavery for all time.'

There followed an uneasy silence. Feet shifted restlessly, eyes expressed doubt, voices muttered against us. I knew frustration, urgent, desperate. I had failed to convince these people. But what more could I say? I felt miserable, filled with doubts of myself.

Yzz-Five took a hand in the game. He called on his helpers to aid him. Waves of mental thought beat at me, terrible in intensity, overwhelming in its insistence. The barrage of thought deepened; power-ful minds were linked, battering at the doubts of the Martians. The aliens showed pictures of what had happened to races in their own universe. They demonstrated the power of thought again and again. They insisted that our story was the true one, that only immediate belief, and action based on that belief, could save the universe. They told of their own rebellion against the Emperor . . .

I was shaking under that broadside of concentrated thought — and I'd had previous experience. The Martians, Ross, and Fisher must have suffered mental agonies they had never imagined possible. I felt sorry for them, but there was no other way. Yzz-Five must have used all his powers to convince them that in starting a war against Earth, Mars was preparing the way for the Emperor.

I moved restlessly. It was impossible to relax in that room. The tension built up to a climax; and stopped. A single thought came:

Do you believe now?

There was a long silence. I looked round the ring of faces and knew we had won the first battle.

It was one of the generals who answered for them all. He said, simply:

'We believe. Tell us what we must do.'

Yzz-Five said: 'I will teleport you back to the surface. You must each use your authority to spread the truth to others. Arrange public broadcasts. Use any means you can to delay the preparations for war: Fight war propaganda wherever you find it. Hold mass meetings; and beware of those in power — remember that the leaders in the government are aliens. I will send you back now.'

I watched him start the teleportation machine. The star-shaped wafers of metal turned faster. Yzz-Five concentrated; and one after another, the Martians disappeared from the room.

I looked at Ross and Fisher, and said:

'Somehow, you must get a message through to Earth. Tell them the whole story. Prevent Earth attacking Mars.'

Then they, too, were gone, and I was alone with Sadie and Yzz-Five. The small man switched off his machine. I found myself doubting that this had really happened.

In that empty room, it seemed incredible. But I had to believe — that was what was so tremendously important.

Yzz-Five said: 'The first step is taken. Without your help, I could not have convinced them. Without mine, you could not. Together, we have triumphed.'

Sadie looked worried.

'Is that going to be enough?' she asked. 'The Emperor's agents will not be long in striking a counter-blow. Do you really think we'll win?'

'We shall win in the end, Miss Lubinski — if we are in time. Time is against us now. But I have another plan which will help defeat the Emperor.'

He crossed to the new machine I had noticed previously, and touched it with his hand.

'This will amplify my thoughts and broadcast them to the people of Mars. Each of my helpers has one. Together, we will send a message of peace, impressing on all the desire to be friends with Earth. In this way, we will undermine the Emperor's wave of hate-thought.'

I studied the machine. It was simply

constructed; a tube of black metal from which wires trailed to a power supply. There was a gauge and a control point; and that was all. I didn't doubt it would behave as Yzz-Five claimed. I had reached the point where I believed in the alien implicitly.

'You'll project — ' I started

And stopped. The floor shifted under my feet. The walls vibrated. Sound waves beat against my ears. The very ground shook and heaved, as if some violent explosion had started off a volcanic eruption far beneath the surface of the planet.

13

Terror!

'Do not be afraid,' Yzz-Five said, confidently. 'Nothing can harm us — the thought screen will hold.'

Sadie clung to me, trembling, her face white. 'What is it, Alec? What's happening?'

My lips were dry and my pulse was racing. I mumbled something about an earthquake and looked to Yzz-Five for the explanation. The small man said:

'I don't know yet. I am trying to find out.'

He sat, concentrated in thought. The walls continued to shake. The floor of our hideaway tilted at an angle. The ground rumbled like an angry giant. I held tight to Sadie and prayed that whatever it was would stop soon. The sound increased in volume, became deafening — through it, I heard Sadie scream as the light failed. It flickered, went out . . . there was darkness and noise and the sensation of being thrown about. It felt as if the whole planet were breaking up.

The light came on again and I saw that Yzz-Five had not moved. The calmness of his face reassured me a little. I detached Sadie's arms from about my neck.

'No need to strangle me,' I said. 'It's all right, now — the quake's passing.'

Some degree of calmness returned to the room as the rumbling lessened and the ground stopped shaking.

'It's over now,' I said. 'Nothing to worry about.'

Yzz-Five looked grave.

'Perhaps it is now that you should worry, Mr. Black. That was no natural eruption. I suspect an atomic explosion. I think we are too late to prevent the war.'

He switched on the vision screen, showing the streets of Marsport. I saw fallen buildings, roads gashed by giant chasms, the dead lying heaped in mounds. I saw that the dome had cracked . . .

Yzz-Five turned another dial and the

excited voice of a radio commentator filled the room: 'Earth spies have struck the first blow in the war! An atom bomb was detonated at the Vestal uranium mines, utterly destroying the whole area. Shock waves set off a quake that wrecked one of the main domes of the city; thousands died instantly. This part of the city has been sealed off and — '

Yzz-Five turned off the sound. He said:

'It is as I feared. The Emperor has been quick to make his counter-blow. This is the spark to set off interplanetary war. We must act at once if we are to do any good.'

I was still staring at the vision screen, horrified by the scenes of devastation it revealed. Not one person was left alive in that section of Marsport. There was no movement of any kind. There were rubble and debris and crashed vehicles, torn bodies and twisted limbs. The silence of death hung over the wreckage and far above, a network of cracks showed in the once airtight dome.

Sadie was moaning softly. I took her in my arms to comfort her. The scene in the vision screen changed, showing another part of the devastated area. The damage was so great it almost defied belief; the death roll would be the largest Mars had ever known. A third of the city of Marsport must have been laid waste.

'How did it happen?' I said. 'No Earth spy — '

'Very simply, Mr. Black.' Yzz-Five's voice had a note of grimness about it. 'I should have thought of this. Agents of the Emperor have teleported an atom bomb into the uranium mines.'

Very simply, I thought. *They teleported an atom bomb* . . . I shuddered, realizing again the power of thought that the Emperor commanded. And Earth would get the blame for this outrage; that was the trigger for releasing the Martians' hatred of Terra. I doubted if anything could stop the war now.

Yzz-Five tuned in to sound again. The commentator came on:

'Martian Intelligence has named the Earth spy responsible for this outrage. He is Alexander Black, masquerading as a writer of space adventure stories. Watch for this spy — he is still at large, still free to carry out the treacherous dictates of his masters, the tyrants of Earth's government. He must be hunted down and killed on sight!'

I was stunned. Sadie gasped in alarm.

The commentator went on: 'Black is being aided by a traitor, a woman, Sadie Lubinski. She, too, must be killed. This pair are dangerous. Every loyal Martian must keep watch for them; when they are found, kill them!'

Sadie looked at me. She said:

'A traitor! This is Lingstrom's doing — '

Yzz-Five nodded.

'An agent of the Emperor posing as Lingstrom,' he corrected. 'The real head of Martian Intelligence is dead, of course. This is the Emperor's way of limiting your freedom of action — also, he hopes to discredit your story if you manage to broadcast it to the people of Mars.'

'This puts us in a spot,' I said, grimly. 'What are we going to do now?'

'Watch.' Yzz-Five moved the dial controlling the vision screen. The scene changed.

I saw a section of the city that had not suffered from the explosion. I saw a crowd of Martians demonstrating their hatred of Earth; I heard the voice of an orator:

'Our dead must be avenged! Earth's dictators must be exterminated before they can strike again. Already, Alexander Black and the traitor woman Lubinski have struck a mortal blow, murdering thousands of innocent people. We cannot afford to wait for the next attack. Our armies are ready, our spaceships loaded with atomic bombs — we must take the war away from Mars, into space, to Earth itself!'

The crowd cheered and stamped. I saw the glint of light on guns. I saw hatred in the faces of men and women. I heard the shouting:

'War against Earth! Carry the war to Earth. Send the ships now, let our bombs rain on their cities — let them feel the might of Mars. Vengeance, and freedom!'

Yzz-Five said: 'The Emperor's agents are using hate-thoughts to work up the emotions of the crowd. Soon they will have a mob lusting for blood, insanely bent on destruction. Then the ships will leave for Earth and there will be nothing we can do.'

Sadie's face was white; her hands clenched into tiny fists.

'The fools! Can't they see it's just a trick? Why — '

She was shaking with anger and fear. I held her close and soothed her.

'Don't blame your people,' I said. 'It's the aliens and their devilish thought-amplifiers. If only there was some way to break their power . . . '

'Before the explosion I was confident of success,' Yzz-Five said slowly. 'Now I am not so sure. Your race is highly emotional, and the death of thousands of Martians a terrible spark to ignite the fires of war. It will not be easy to persuade them that Earth was not to blame.'

He turned the control dial again and again. Each time I saw a new scene of Marsport, different yet the same. In every part of the city, crowds were gathering to demand war against Earth. Again and again I saw mass demonstrations and heard the propaganda of war. Even with the volume control tuned down, the sound of shouting filled our hideaway; and, always, it was the same:

'Death to Earthmen! Avenge our dead. Wipe out the murderers, blast their planet to fragments, Send the ships to Earth and bomb their cities. Let them know the terror of atomic war!'

I felt sick with terror. There was sweat on my face and an emptiness in my stomach. It seemed to me now that there could be no hope of beating the aliens. Sadie and I were hunted; we would be killed on sight. And war between Earth and Mars was imminent, inevitable. The Emperor's invasion would go unchecked . . .

I knew an inner conflict of loyalties. Reason told me I had to stand by the Martians no matter what happened; only in that way could we beat the aliens. And Sadie was Martian — I could not turn against her. Yet, looking at the scene in the vision screen, I felt my emotional ties to Earth. This was war and I am an Earthman . . . I must stand by my own planet. I was an agent for Terran Intelligence and had sworn allegiance to that planet.

'Destroy the tyrants!' came the roar of the crowd. 'Level their cities to the ground and avenge our dead. Death to Earthmen. Send the ships now — atom-bombs for Earth!'

I heard the beat of drums, muffled, throbbing a monotonous rhythm. I heard the chant of thousands:

'*War . . . war . . . war!*'

I reacted to it. Mars was the enemy. I had to get a message through to Earth, to warn my own people. They must be prepared to meet the Martian ships, to beat off these madmen. Nothing mattered except saving Earth from utter annihilation.

I turned on Yzz-Five and said, urgently:

'Teleport me to the radio station — I must get word through to Earth.'

Yzz-Five looked at me and said nothing. There was a look of pity in his eyes.

Sadie snapped: 'You can't do that, Alec. You can't desert now. If Earth were warned, they would send a fleet of spaceships to Mars and — '

'You suggest I should let my people be wiped out without a chance?'

'No, not that, Alec. But don't you see, if Earth is warned, it means the end of the Mars colony. We can't stand against the superior force of Earth — '

I pointed at the vision screen. 'They think so! Listen to them shouting for blood.'

Sadie said: 'They can't help it, you know that. The Emperor has tricked them, filled their minds with hatred and the desire to kill. If they could think clearly — '

I pounced on the point.

'But they can't! Look at them, wild animals lusting to kill — and you want me to let that pack loose on Earth, without warning. I won't. Get me to the radio station, Yzz-Five — Mars must take its chance of survival!'

Sadie clawed at my arms.

'No, Alec. You know what it means if you do. The ships of Earth will obliterate all life from my planet. It's my people you're planning to murder. I hate you when you talk like this. It's always been the same to Earthmen — might is right. It's all you understand. I'll force you to stay here!'

She clung to me with all her strength. I tried to shake her off, but couldn't. I lost my temper and hit out at her.

'Leave me alone,' I snarled. 'I must get a warning to Earth.'

Sadie fell back as I struck her. She was crying, and I felt ashamed — but I knew that what I must do was right. I said, grimly:

'Yzz-Five. Start your machine and get me out of here.'

'No!' Sadie came back at me. 'Don't. Yzz-Five — don't!'

I would have hit her again, only the small man took a hand in the game. Suddenly, I was unable to move. I stood, paralysed, and saw that Sadie was also motionless. Yzz-Five had impressed his will on us both. The thought came:

You are both wrong. In giving in to your emotions, you are helping the Emperor. He is deliberately striving to widen the gulf between Mars and Earth.

201

The only hope for both your worlds is in sticking together. You must help each other to fight the Emperor. Only by avoiding war can the invasion be stopped.

Yzz-Five released us from telepathic bondage. Sanity returned to me.

I said: 'You're right, Yzz-Five. Thanks.'

Sadie said: 'I'm sorry, Alec. It was my fault.'

'War against Earth!' screamed the crowd in the vision screen.

It irritated me. I turned to Yzz-Five, and snapped:

'For heaven's sake, switch that thing off. I can't stand any more of it.'

He switched it off.

'You must remain calm,' he said. 'This trouble will pass. Now, quiet please — I must concentrate my thoughts to broadcast a message of peace to the people of Mars.'

I watched him settle before the black metal tube. He operated the controls.

Time passed slowly in the hideaway. We waited for Yzz-Five to finish, imagining the amplifier projecting a powerful thought-wave to combat the Emperor's hate-broadcast. All over Mars, helpers of Yzz-Five would be seated before similar machines, adding the power of their minds to the message.

I felt restless, unable to settle. While I waited, the first ships might be blasting off to drop their bombs on Earth cities. I did not like admitting there was nothing I could do to help. This was a battle between minds; a battle fought with the power of telepathy, mechanically amplified — a silent, unceasing battle between Yzz-Five and the Emperor.

Sadie laid her hand on my forehead.

'Try to rest, Alec,' she said softly. 'We can only wait — and pray.'

After a time, Yzz-Five looked up from the thought amplifier. He said:

'The agents of the Emperor are too powerful for my limited forces. We cannot break the hate-broadcast unaided. We will try again, when those Martians whom we have instructed in the truth, speak to the people.'

He used the vision screen again. I saw larger crowds on the streets of Marsport.

I saw demonstrations calling for immediate war against Earth. I heard voices raised in hatred and saw faces flushed with the desire to kill. A procession formed, winding through the main thoroughfares, gathering in numbers; it moved slowly, resolutely towards the spaceport where rocket ships were being loaded with fuel and bombs. I saw an army preparing to go to war.

There was a lump in my throat, a tension in my body. I felt sick with horror. If this was not stopped . . . I had to keep telling myself the Martians were not in control of their senses. I had to hang on to the idea that we must pull together if the Emperor were to be defeated. It was not easy, imagining what would happen to Earth if these ships left Mars.

Sadie clung to me, her eyes pleading with me.

'Wait, Alec. You must have faith.'

I remembered my experience with the Emperor, how I had tried so hard to convince the Martians of the truth. Had my efforts been wasted? Why didn't they speak up?

Yzz-Five said: 'It will not be easy for them. The devastation of their principal city, apparently by an Earth spy, will not make the Martians very willing to listen. It will take a brave man to speak out now.'

I waited, watching the dreadful scenes in the vision screen, My throat was dry. Why didn't something happen? Surely one of those who had been teleported to the hideaway would make an appeal? Surely —

Sadie said: 'Yzz-Five. Teleport me to the radio station. I will tell the people the truth.'

Yzz-Five shook his head.

'You are branded a traitor. Miss Lubinski. You would be killed instantly, without a chance to tell your story.'

Then the radio came alive. It was the general who had spoken for the Martians after Yzz-Five had used all his telepathic powers to convince them of the truth. He spoke, slowly and emphatically:

'People of Mars, listen to me. You have been tricked into thinking you want war, tricked by a race of aliens whose purpose it is to invade our universe. The people of

Earth are our friends. It is the aliens, masquerading as Martians in authority, who are the enemy. Listen carefully and — '

He went on to repeat the story he had been told by Yzz-Five and myself. I listened in admiration, wondering how he had managed to get control of the radio station — how he kept his voice on the air for all to hear. I was proud of that general.

Yzz-Five was back at his thought-amplifier. He and his helpers would be broadcasting thoughts of peace to break the Emperor's rule of hate. The general's voice droned on; Yzz-Five spoke with the silence of thought. I waited, and wondered: Could they bring the Martians to their senses in time?

14

The only way

The tension of those long minutes of waiting became unbearable. I stood before the vision screen, rigid as a stone figure, my hands clenched. Tiny drops of moisture trickled down my face. My heart was pounding and I could hear my breath hissing as I breathed.

Yzz-Five sat, relaxed, before the black tube that was the thought-amplifier. He maintained the illusion of being a small, nondescript man, dressed in a grey suit, and I was glad of that. I did not want to see his alien form.

The air in the hideaway seemed charged with electricity. The radiance appeared harsher, the shadows cast by the strange machines harder. The bare walls echoed with the general's voice from the sound box.

' . . . all government officials must be

forced to submit to a thought-test carried out by Yzz-Five and his helpers,' he was saying. 'Only in this way can we rid ourselves of those who would betray us. You must not go to war against Earth. The Emperor and his agents are the true enemy . . .'

The general's voice went on and on. The tension built up in that small cell till I thought I should scream. The silent battle of minds raged unceasingly. In the vision screen, Martians clamoured for war . . .

Abruptly, the general's voice stopped in the middle of a sentence. Sadie's copper eyes widened in fear. 'What's happened to the general?' she asked hoarsely.

I licked my lips nervously; my gaze turned towards Yzz-Five. The small man looked up from his machine and his eyes held a hopelessness I had never thought to see there.

'I can do nothing,' he said. 'The Emperor's agents are too powerful.'

'The general?'

Yzz-Five concentrated again, directing a probing beam of thought at the radio station. After a short pause, he said:

'The general is dead. Agents of the Emperor sent a mob to kill him.'

Sadie said, in a whisper: 'We must stop them. We must be able to do something.'

The radio came alive again, crackling with the voice of officialdom.

'Another traitor has been eliminated. General Kegan. whose voice you heard broadcasting a few minutes ago, has paid for his treachery. Take no notice of the fantastic story he told; it is no more than a fiction invented by the Earth spy, Alexander Black. Black and the woman Lubinski are still free — search them out and deal with them. Other traitors in Earth's pay are known. Some have already paid the penalty; others — '

I was looking at the vision screen. I saw the President of the Martian Women's Council — one of those who had learnt the truth from Yzz-Five — dragged through the streets. She was a tall, well-built woman with flowing black hair. Her clothes had been torn from her, and her body was stained with blood.

She was shouting, but her words were

drowned by the animal noises of those who held her. I watched as she was forced to her knees, beaten with rods and guns till she lay dead on the ground.

The voice of the commentator said: 'Thus die all traitors to our magnificent cause. None must be allowed to stand in our way. Death to Earthmen. Seek them out now. Our ships are ready to leave for Earth!'

'War . . . war . . . war!' chanted the mob, swaying in bestial frenzy.

Sadie was sobbing.

'It can't be true,' she moaned. 'It can't!'

I held Sadie close, thinking that if it were not for Yzz-Five's protective screen, we might ourselves be acting like wild animals. It was a horrifying thought.

The radio spoke again: 'Earth spies have sent a message to Earth. Spaceships loaded with atomic bombs are on the way to blast our planet. Do not fear — our ships are ready. We will clear them from space and go on to settle with the tyrants who would enslave us forever. See, the Earth ships approach!'

The scene in the vision screen changed

once more. I saw the black void of space and red dots of light; red dots that moved steadily nearer, heralding Earth's armada. Fisher or Ross must have got a message through. I wondered if either of them were still alive; and doubted it.

'Nothing can stop the war now,' I said.

Yzz-Five looked worried. 'We still have a few hours left,' he said, 'before the battle starts — but I cannot see what is to be done. My telepathic powers are limited, weaker than those of the Emperor. I fear that my interference has resulted only in an increased restlessness of the Martian people. They doubt — and to quell their doubt, must indulge in violence.'

The ships of Earth disappeared from the screen and, again, I saw the streets of Marsport. Men and women were running wild, shouting:

'Seek out the Earthmen and destroy them. Death . . . death . . . death . . . '

I saw Earthmen dragged from hiding and killed. It was like a scene from a nightmare; there was no mercy in the faces of the Martians. They hunted in packs, ransacking the offices and shops where Earthmen worked. The luckless few were hounded to the streets and brutally murdered. All Mars responded to the thought-waves of hatred sent out by the Emperor's agents.

'Kill, kill, kill!' came the dread chant of thousands of voices, while, in the background, the rhythmic throb of drums pounded unceasingly.

Sadie covered her eyes, turning away from the scenes of carnage. I swore, shaking with cold, helpless fury.

Yzz-Five said, gravely: 'The war fever is mounting. The Emperor's agents have done their work well.' He shook his head, sighing. 'I will try once more to break the hate broadcast.'

He returned to the black tube and switched on the power. I held Sadie, her face buried in my coat, and watched the screen. Now I saw a view of the spacefield and its rows of rocket ships. Men were working feverishly, loading equipment and bombs and fuel; how long before they blasted off to engage the Terran armada?

Yzz-Five remained silent, concentrated

in thought over the amplifier. In other hideaways, his helpers would be sending out the same telepathic impulse in an attempt to break the Emperor's hold over the people of Mars. It seemed a hopeless task.

There was a fresh scene on the screen. I recognized the gaunt figure of the mathematician who had grasped the idea of dimensional worlds. He was standing on a balcony overlooking one of the main avenues of Marsport.

He shouted: 'Listen to me! General Kegan told you the truth — there are aliens in our midst, posing as government officials. They want this war with Earth to hide their own invasion of our universe. Stop this rioting before it is too late. The aliens come from another world, far across the dimensions. I will try to explain this to — '

I heard the shot. The mathematician doubled in sudden agony, hands clasped to his breast. I saw the blood seep between his fingers. Then he fell.

The official commentator returned to the air:

'One more traitor has been eliminated. Pay no attention to his mad ravings — he was in the pay of the Earth spy, Alexander Black. Black and the traitor Lubinski are still at large. Redouble your efforts to find them. They must be killed on sight!'

I shivered at the venom with which the words were delivered.

Sadie muttered: 'The Emperor must still be afraid we can stop him if he takes this trouble over us.'

'I doubt it,' I said, bitterly. 'More likely we're being used as a decoy to prevent your people thinking too deeply — all the time they've a quarry to hunt, they won't stop to reason things out for themselves.'

The vision screen showed the blackness of space again. The red flares of the rocket trails were nearer. I counted thirty ships, star-bright against the dark void between the planets. And there would be more following.

The commentator said: 'See, the enemy approach! Do not be alarmed, people of Mars; soon our spaceships will rise to attack the might of Earth. We will sweep them from the skies. Our bombs will fall on the cities of Earth in endless stream, leaving not one of the tyrant race alive. Mars will triumph as surely as night follows day!'

'The fools!' There were tears in Sadie's eyes. 'Can't they see that Earth must win in the end? Our colonies are under airtight domes; once the domes are shattered . . . why can't they see their danger?'

Earth must win; I knew that — but thousands would die first, and the alien invasion would be established on Mars. It was the beginning of the end, not only for the human race, but for the races of all planets in our universe. There was a lump in my throat. I looked towards Yzz-Five as he sat over his thought-amplifier. Could he do nothing to stop the Emperor's forces?

The small man turned away from his machine with a sigh.

'Useless,' he said. 'The degree of amplification that I and my helpers can achieve is nothing compared to that of the Emperor's agents. More and more of them have crossed the dimensions from

Yzzolda — and each adds his mind to the hate broadcast. Our group is too small to stand against them.'

We stood, helpless, watching the vision screen. There was the sickness of fear deep inside me. The battle was going to the enemy and there seemed nothing we could do. Or was there one last, desperate chance?

I took a deep breath and looked at Sadie. I saw from her expression that she had the same idea. I turned to Yzz-Five, and said:

'Teleport us to the radio station. We will broadcast together. We must try to stop this war.'

Sadie added: 'Perhaps, together, we can convince my people. You must help us to make the attempt. Don't you see, it's the one hope now. It's that — or complete subjugation to the Emperor.'

Yzz-Five remained silent, regarding us thoughtfully.

'Your sacrifice would be wasted,' he said at last. 'You would be killed before you uttered one word.'

I thought he was probably right, but

the scenes in the vision screen convinced me we had to try. My lips were dry. I wet them with my tongue. I said:

'It's a chance we'll have to take. Start your machine, Yzz-Five.'

He studied us again, and I thought I detected admiration in his eyes. Admiration — or pity.

'Very well,' he said, and crossed to the teleportation machine. 'Prepare yourselves for the transmission.'

I looked at Sadie for a long moment, It might be our last time together, but I tried not to think about that.

'I love you.' I said. 'I love you so very much, Sadie.'

'It could have been so wonderful. Alec,' she whispered, clinging to me. 'It could — '

'Now!' said Yzz-Five.

We braced ourselves. I saw the bare walls of the hideaway, the small man crouched over his machine with the star-shaped metal pieces. I saw a brightly lit studio, control panels, a microphone hookup. And Martians armed with guns. We were in the radio station.

Sadie began to run for a microphone. I followed, knowing in my heart that we'd never make it. Death was only seconds away. The Martians spotted us. Their eyes were hostile; their guns swung to cover us. I saw a thin man with a pointed beard and staring eyes. Lingstrom! He was there, waiting for us. We had walked into a trap.

Lingstrom raised his arm, pointing at us. He said, in his flat, emotionless voice:

'Mr. Black — and Miss Lubinski. I thought you would come into the open if I waited long enough. You will not escape this time. Martians — kill them!'

I stared into the muzzles of guns. I saw trigger fingers tighten. There was noise, and flashes, and . . .

Yzz-Five said, quietly: 'You see? It was useless. Your deaths would have gained us nothing.'

We were in the underground hideaway again. It was anticlimax. At the moment of approaching death I had lost my fear; now, I trembled. Sadie was hysterical.

'You might have let us die trying. You might have allowed us that. What can we look forward to now? Mental slavery for the rest of our lives.'

I took her by the shoulders and shook her.

'Stop it, Sadie! While we're alive, there's hope. We'll find a way to beat them yet.'

I sat down, weak and shaking with anger.

'I suppose we can escape to another planet,' Sadie said. 'We'll have a short while together, Alec.'

'Yes, flee to another world before the advance of the Emperor. Then to another — and another. Running all the time, waiting for the aliens to catch up with us. That's no life for any human being, Terran or Martian. We must stand and fight — or die.'

Yzz-Five said: 'Truly your race has many admirable qualities. Perhaps if the races on the worlds of my own universe had been as determined to resist subjuga- tion, then the Emperor's power would be considerably less than it is.'

I was not convinced.

'We don't seem able to defend

ourselves very well,' I said with bitterness. 'Look at the way the Martians have gone under to his telepathic powers.'

I stared at the vision screen as I spoke and the scenes there took the heart out of me. An army was marching towards the spaceport, ready to embark for Earth. The cheering mob almost drowned out the strains of martial music to which the men marched. Silver rockets, noses pointed to the sky, waited in readiness.

Yzz-Five said: 'Tell me, Mr. Black, and Miss Lubinski, is there nothing your people would not suffer to resist subjugation? No hardship, no sacrifice? Is there — '

'Nothing!' I answered him.

He paused, studying us a long time. Then he said:

'There may be a way. It is dangerous, but it might work. It is the only way left open to me to break the Emperor's power. Your people will suffer such agony that . . . ' He hesitated, and, for a moment, the alienness of him looked out from those pale eyes. He seemed, desperately, to be trying to understand something about us.

'It must be for you to decide,' he finished. 'The effect will be more terrible than you can imagine. Insanity . . . or worse . . . perhaps for the whole race.'

I understood then what it was he intended.

I said: 'You are going to reveal the natural form of the aliens. That's what you mean, isn't it?'

He nodded.

'Yes, Mr. Black, that is what I mean. I can break the illusion of the Emperor's agents, revealing them for what they are. It will be a terrible shock, greater even than you think. But it is the only way.'

I knew what my answer was, but it was for Sadie to speak. It was her people who would suffer. We both looked at her.

'You can do this?' she asked. 'I mean, your power is enough to break their thought screen? You weren't able to beat the broadcast of hate.'

'This is different. Before, our energy was dispersed. Now, all my helpers will concentrate on breaking the thought screen of one of the enemy. I don't doubt we will succeed.'

Sadie's face was marble white. I could almost see the struggle going on in her mind. To sacrifice her people so that other races in the universe might be saved . . . to sacrifice them to save Earth. 'Yes,' she said. 'If it is the only way.'

15

The last struggle

I found myself imagining what would happen when Yzz-Five destroyed the aliens' thought-illusion, and the Martians saw them as they really were. I shuddered as I visualized the possible effects this would have. I remembered the fleeting glimpse I had received of the aliens' true form, on Yzzolda — and how intensely I had wanted not to see.

I dare not look at Sadie's face, afraid of what I might see there. In the vision screen, a frenzied mob of Martians surged through the streets of the domed city. An army marched on the spaceport. Rocket ships waited for takeoff.

The mob chanted to the rhythm of drums: 'War — war — war against Earth!'

The scene changed again. The blackness of space filled the screen, dotted with the tell-tale flares of rocket exhausts.

Earth's armada rushed nearer with each second . . . and the aliens waited for the clash, knowing that out of the conflict they would subjugate a universe. Yes, I thought, it is the only way.

Sadie said: 'Don't wait any longer, Yzz-Five. We haven't much time. Do what you must.'

The small man replied: 'I have sent a message to my helpers. We are ready.'

He pointed to the screen.

'Do you see the officer at the head of the column? The officer leading the Martian army to the spaceships? He is an alien. We have selected him for our purpose.'

I studied the man at the head of the army. He looked every inch a military man, dressed in a brightly coloured uniform, his chest almost obscured by glittering medals. He held his head high in the air and swung his arms with the precision of a professional soldier. He was the sort of officer that men would follow without doubting; he had authority implicit in his step and bearing.

I judged that Yzz-Five's selection was

the right one. This disguised alien was at the head of the army; he was between the Martians and their spaceships; and he was in full view of thousands. It was going to be hell let loose when his screen went down and something else lay revealed.

Yzz-Five said: 'We are starting now.'

Sadie crossed to my side and we stood together, staring at the screen.

'It has to be this way.' I said quietly. 'It's for the best.'

My words were clichés, platitudes, meaningless, but I could find nothing better in that moment. Sadie smiled wanly and said nothing. I could feel the tension build up.

The alien at the head of the column faltered in his stride; he recovered himself. I could sense powerful thought-waves converging on him to break his screen. He must be aware of the attack, desperately trying to save himself, to maintain the illusion of being a human. Again his step faltered, and, this time, he did not recover.

The men behind broke step, piling up in disordered ranks. The crowd surged about them. The alien had stopped now; he concentrated his mind for the battle of wills. The army disintegrated into a rabble, uncertain, leaderless. Those at the rear pushed forward, not realizing what was happening.

Yzz-Five said: 'He knows what we are about. He is trying to contact other agents of the Emperor, to get help. We have formed a thought barrier, shutting him off from their aid. He must fight alone.'

An uproar broke loose in the streets; a jumbled mass of Martians surged to and fro, chanting their monotonous dirge:

'War — war — war against Earth!'

And, in the background, the drums pounded incessantly. Yzz-Five's attack went on relentlessly. Beams of concentrated thought hammered at the alien's telepathic illusion. Staring at the screen, I thought I detected a wavering of his image . . . it seemed as if his outline subtly changed. Then he was, again, an officer in the Martian army.

The very air seemed charged with power. I imagined how that alien must feel, completely alone, cut-off from his kind and subjected to a terrific mental barrage. He would fight back with every ounce of willpower he could muster, draining his resources to the breaking point.

He stood alone, stiff and unmoving, silent as he battled to save himself. Martians backed away from him, scared of something they did not understand. Men formed a ring round him, staring at him, muttering amongst themselves. He did not answer when they called to him.

The minutes dragged out. The struggle went on, a score of minds storming a lone citadel, seeking to break the thought-image. I could feel the strain as mental forces greater than anything I had imagined clashed in grim fury. It was as if high-tension cables unleashed their power on one tiny insulator.

Yzz-Five said: 'He is weakening. Soon the illusion will go. Do not look at the screen now.'

I had to force my gaze from the scene in the vision screen, from that still figure ringed by a hushed crowd. The fascination of it gripped me — yet I dare not look longer for fear of losing my sanity. I turned away. Sadie still stared at the screen, as if mesmerized. I grasped her shoulders and dragged her away, covering her eyes.

Yzz-Five said: 'The screen is going — now!'

I was sweating, imagining what must be happening out there on the streets — the last desperate struggle of the alien to retain his illusion . . . and failing. The concentrated telepathic power of Yzz-Five and his helpers would be too much for him. The screen must go down . . . revealing — what?

There came a long, drawn out sigh from the crowd. Then utter silence, stunned, shocked, and I knew it was over. I heard a sound, like that of a damned soul; it was inhuman, terrible, and I tried to block the sound from my ears.

The screaming started, the screaming of thousands of Martians, harrowing, frightful. It went on and on, reaching a climax of insane panic. I glimpsed the screen from the corner of my eye. The crowd had gone berserk. I saw a flurry of arms as madmen tore something to pieces with their bare hands.

Sadie was limp in my arms. She had fainted. I lowered her into a chair, and turned, bracing myself, to look into the vision screen. I could see little detail. The street was one mass of surging, screaming people; of the alien, I saw only fragments of some monstrous body that had been ripped to shreds and trampled into the ground.

Yzz-Five said: 'The shock drove them to destroy the alien — it was the only way they could get rid of the sight that blasted their minds. There will be no war now, Mr. Black; the hatred has gone.'

I nodded, too numb to speak. I stood staring at the screen, aghast at the sight I saw there, shivering at the sounds I heard. The screaming had not stopped. It swelled in volume, a sound empty of reason. All those who had seen the alien were insane. They ran wildly, their mouths open, their eyes glazed with the light of stark horror. Truly, there could be no war now.

Bodies lay on the ground, broken and bleeding. Hundreds must have been crushed in the panic, fallen, trampled on. The streets emptied, but the wailing went on. I could not detect one piece of what might have been the alien's body; he had been completely obliterated.

Madmen rushed through the streets. They ran into walls as if blind, and fell. They were crushed under cars driven by men without sanity. They lay on the ground and kicked their legs. They huddled in corners, whimpering . . .

'Turn it off!' I said, hoarsely. 'I can't take any more.'

Yzz-Five switched off the vision screen. There was silence in the hideaway. I looked at the still figure of Sadie, slumped in the chair, and felt afraid for her.

'I'm glad she didn't see the worst,' I said. 'It'll be bad enough when she realizes what has happened. I must get her out of this — right away from Mars.'

'That would be best,' Yzz-Five assented. 'The danger is past. The people of Mars have received a shock they will never forget. The Emperor is beaten.'

'But the others. Yzz-Five? Will you reveal the other agents of the Emperor?'

I dreaded his reply, thinking what new terror this might bring, and was relieved when he said:

'No, that will not be necessary. The Emperor is not a fool. He knows he has lost now that his invasion is exposed; he does not have the material weapons with which to fight back. Already, his forces have returned to Yzzolda. They will not bother the races of your universe again.'

Sadie recovered consciousness in time to hear his words.

She murmured: 'We've won, then? Beaten the Emperor, Alec?'

I took her in my arms to comfort her.

'Yes, darling,' I said. 'It's over — we've won. The Emperor will never hold us in mental slavery.'

She smiled through the tears that ran down her cheeks.

'And my people?' she asked. 'The people of Mars — what of them?'

I didn't know what to say. My mouth was dry. It was Yzz-Five who answered her.

'Many of your race are insane, and will never recover. That is the price of freedom. Others, who did not see the form of the alien, still live to help those unfortunates, and to carry on the traditions of your people. The sacrifice has been great; but I believe that future generations will uphold your decision, that they will say the price was not too high to pay.'

'You must believe that, Sadie,' I said. 'We had no choice — this was forced upon us, remember that. I'm going to marry you very soon, and take you away from Mars, somewhere you'll have the chance to forget all this. I'm going to spend the rest of my life making you happy.'

Yzz-Five switched on the vision screen again. I saw, not the streets of Marsport, but the dark void of space — and the flaring jets of the Earth fleet. The ships were very close now, reminding me I still had one job left to do.

I kissed Sadie, and said:

'Wait for me, darling, I shan't be gone long.' I looked at Yzz-Five. 'Teleport me to the radio station. I have to stop those ships dropping their bombs.'

He started the teleportation machine.

'Ready, Mr. Black? I will transmit you to the radio station and, this time, you will encounter no opposition.'

Sadie said, determinedly: 'I'm coming with you, Alec.'

Yzz-Five nodded.

'It is best. I shall send you both back to the surface, then return to Yzzolda. This is goodbye, Mr. Black.'

Somehow I hadn't expected our parting to come like that. I'd imagined something more formal, a triumphal banquet, Yzz-Five shaking hands with the leaders of Earth's government. I was so used to seeing him as a small man in a grey suit that it came as a shock to remember that he was in reality identical with the horror that had driven thousands of Martians completely out of their minds. But he, too, had made a sacrifice, fighting against his own race to save another universe.

I said, simply: 'You have the gratitude of our people, Yzz-Five.'

He answered: 'The battle, for me, is not over. The Emperor will try to invade the worlds of other dimensions. I must help them, too.'

I regarded him with new respect, unable to find the words to express my feelings. The metal star-shapes were revolving at high speed; we had not long together.

Yzz-Five spoke for the last time:

'The spirit of your race has given me new heart. I, and my helpers, will not rest until the Emperor's power is broken. You may be proud of your part in this . . . and now, goodbye, my friends. I return to my own world.'

Sadie called: 'Goodbye, Yzz-Five — and good luck.'

The hideaway vanished. Sadie and I stood once more in the radio station. It was deserted now, the microphones waiting for us. I switched on the power and spoke into a microphone.

'Alexander Black calling the Terran fleet. Answer please — this is urgent.' I gave my security number and repeated my request.

A familiar voice said: 'Go ahead, Alec. What is the situation on Mars?'

It was the chief. I knew a sudden surge of relief; till then, I had not felt certain I could convince those aboard the Earth ships. Now I knew it would be all right.

I said: 'Listen, chief, you've got to stop the fleet from attacking Mars. There will be no war. One third of the population of Marsport is dead, another third insane. Those that are left need your help urgently — this is a time for Earth to forget past quarrels and come as a friend.'

The chief listened without comment as I gave him a broad outline of the alien invasion. I left the details for later.

'Wait,' he said.

'It's going to be all right,' I told Sadie.

The chief wasn't gone long. I imagined he had some important people aboard and was convincing them that my word was good.

His voice came back through the loudspeaker: 'We understand the situation, Alec. You and Miss Lubinski have done well. You can tell the people of Mars that our ships will land within the hour, and that we shall give them all the help we can. You can tell them that Earth is their friend in this time of distress. The people of Mars have the sympathy of every Earthman; we are proud of our colonists.'

The air went dead. Sadie took the microphone to broadcast to her people.

'Martians! Do not be afraid when the Earth ships land. They come as friends, to help us. The threat of invasion is over — the aliens have gone back to their own world across the dimensions. Welcome the Earthmen, for we need their aid. A new era is starting, in which the peoples of Mars and Earth will join in peace and freedom.'

It was all over. An hour later, the fleet landed and men of Earth set about rebuilding the colony that had taken three generations to establish. I made a full report to the chief and obtained leave of absence . . .

. . . A month passed. I married Sadie Lubinski and took her to the pleasure resort of Mercury for our honeymoon. We were happy enough, but always, there was that shadow between us — the shadow of a dreadful responsibility. It had taken me a long time to persuade Sadie to leave Mars; even then she had left only because her doctor ordered it.

She maintained it was her duty to remain amongst those she had sacrificed to insanity, and to help them as far as she could. I did my best to take my share of the responsibility from her shoulders — but she was a Martian, and I a man of Earth. They were her people, not mine. I understood then how far apart the colony had grown from the mother planet.

It was useless to argue with her. She agreed there had been no other course left open for us to take. She agreed that anything was better than subjugation to the Emperor. She agreed that Mars would rise to new heights of glory through the terrible sacrifice of her people . . . then she would see one of the unfortunates and a great sadness would come to her eyes.

I knew, as we basked in the sun baths of Mercury, that this thing would always be between us. It could not destroy our love — nothing could do that — but, always, the shadow would be there. She would look into the sky and I knew she was longing to return to her own planet.

On the last day of our honeymoon, she said, 'You know what it is I must do. Alec. I cannot ask you to share such a life. You must go your way, and I mine.'

'The responsibility is as much mine as yours,' I said. 'We will go together, and work amongst those who gave their reason so that a universe might be free. And our children will continue the work.'

She nodded and I knew that she had accepted my decision.

I tore up the opening chapters of *Vendetta on Mars*. The true Mars Story would never be published; that would remain in the archives of the Intelligence Service, marked TOP SECRET.

Together, we boarded a spaceship bound for Mars.

THE END

We do hope that you have enjoyed reading this large print book.

Did you know that all of our titles are available for purchase?

We publish a wide range of high quality large print books including:
Romances, Mysteries, Classics
General Fiction
Non Fiction and Westerns

Special interest titles available in large print are:
The Little Oxford Dictionary
Music Book, Song Book
Hymn Book, Service Book

Also available from us courtesy of Oxford University Press:
Young Readers' Dictionary
(large print edition)
Young Readers' Thesaurus
(large print edition)

For further information or a free brochure, please contact us at:
Ulverscroft Large Print Books Ltd.,
The Green, Bradgate Road, Anstey,
Leicester, LE7 7FU, England.
Tel: (00 44) 0116 236 4325
Fax: (00 44) 0116 234 0205

Other titles in the
Linford Mystery Library:

PROJECT JOVE

John Glasby

Norbert Donner and Project Director Stanton work on Project Jove, observing the robots in the Jupiter surface lab by means of the Fly, a remote-controlled exploratory ship. Then Senator Clinton Durant arrives from earth convinced Stanton is hiding something on Jupiter's surface. And, unconvinced of dire warnings of danger, he and his assistants ride a Fly down to question the surface lab robots. They soon find themselves completely at the mercy of the giant planet and its devastating storms . . .

THE STELLAR LEGION

E. C. Tubb

Wilson, a waif of the war of unity, spends his boyhood in forced labour. When he is sent to the penal world of Stellar, he survives, winning promotion in the Stellar Legion, a brutal military system. Laurance, Director of the Federation of Man, wants to dissolve the Legion. He pits his wits against its commander, Hogarth. He's terrified lest the human wolves, trained and hardened in blood and terror, should ravage the defenceless galaxy . . .

ENDLESS DAY

John Russell Fearn

It's June 30th. And in Annex 10, situated in the Adirondack Mountains of New York, scientist Dr. Gray and his team can hardly believe their instrument readings. It's four o'clock, and as the seconds pass, they see that chaos looms for mankind. The Earth is growing hotter, temperatures rocket, as the sun shines through the night and causes endless days. Everyone suffers — the rich, the poor, the criminal and the family man. Will it ever end?